NEW RIVER
Gorge(ous)

NEW RIVER Gorge (ous)

OLIVIA HOPE McCARTHY

To the reader who wonders where their place is in the world.
This one is for you.

Content Warning

The following story contains mentions of themes that some readers
may be sensitive to:

- being left at the altar
- trichotillomania and anxiety
- concern for potential mental decline of an older character
- brief mention of pregnancy out of wedlock (in past)
-brief mention of adoption (in past)
- pregnancy (side character) and brief mention of fertility struggles

*"The parks are the Nation's pleasure grounds
and the Nation's restoring places..."*

—J. Horace McFarland (1916)

1

BROOKE

Red paint splatters the floor of my apartment, and I can't help but notice the way the liquid makes a pattern. It looks like blood. Like this place is a murder scene. It's fitting, really. My tombstone will say, 'Here lies Brooke Belle Bastion, beloved twin and serial killer of relationships.'

Dramatic much? Yes. But I don't care. I'm allowing myself to not care for twenty-four hours. I'll lose myself in ice cream topped with M&M's and hot fudge. Matt will call tomorrow at eleven a.m. after his gym sessions, and I'll tell him then. He'll come over, and we'll eat more junk together, and he'll let me watch *Is it Cake?* until everything looks like cake and we're crazed enough to think we could make hyperrealistic cakes ourselves. We'll speak in the 'twin' language that no one else understands, and we'll attempt to make a cake in the shape of a random household object.

Matt will text Mom a picture of the object and said cake (which will not look at all like the object because we're both terrible bakers), and she'll laugh, and then he'll leave to get dinner and work on his business after asking three times in 'twin' if I'm ok. I'll smile and shove a fistful of the cake in my mouth and assure him that I am. I'll be lying, but I'll also be ready to be alone by then.

Life will go on for everyone else, so why worry them? I've got it completely under control. I'll be cheerful and in charge and not at all bothered by the fact that I had to break off yet another relationship because of … reasons.

I scrub a hand down my face and feel the sticky red paint adhere to my skin. Great, now I look bloody.

I stand up from the easel and retrieve the paintbrush I accidentally knocked to the floor as I let sobs shake my body.

The anxiety I muster through regularly rears its ugly head.

Totally alone, I can finally let things bother me. And I am bothered. Bothered that I can't find a man to match my love for adventures, a man to challenge me, to *love me*—the messy parts and all. Bothered that my personality has earned me the nickname 'the general' and that no man I've attempted a relationship with has been willing to match my zest for life and penchant for … directing situations because the alternative is not knowing what's going to happen.

I'm good at being in charge. I know that. But wouldn't it be nice if a man, romantically involved with me, could sometimes at least *try*? I'm the opposite of a pushover, but everyone I've ever dated cows to my personality, or assumes I'm a conquest.

I'm too big. Too bright. Too forceful. And I try to tone it down, but somehow I always choose the dates, the restaurants, the movies, the adventures. I get the sense that I make it too easy for other people to follow. I'm decisive, but not many people are, so it feels weird. I wish I knew what to do differently.

I stand and march to the painting supply drawer under my kitchen sink. I grab an old paint-splattered towel and return to clean up the mess. I'm crouched down on my heels, wiping up the murder scene of Brooke and Stanford's relationship, when my phone buzzes with an incoming call, startling me.

My elbow slips, and I crash into the leg of the easel. I grab the leg to stop it from tipping, but it's not enough. The palette flies off its perch and whacks me on the forehead, and paint specks cover everything.

My phone flies off the ledge of the easel and miraculously lands face-up in the mess. I snarl at it, but it's Matt, so I slide the video call on and bark out a 'What!?' in greeting.

Matt is unperturbed by my gruff greeting. "Hey, sis." His eyes travel down my face, taking in my paint-covered state. He chuckles. "What happened?"

I launch into the whole story about how Stanford Jopman is not the man for me. How he picked me up for the date I asked him to plan and he waggled his eyebrows and said, 'Oh, I planned it alright.' Then he insinuated something extremely crude and not at all what I wanted to do with him, or what I meant when I asked him to plan our date.

Matt's jaw clenches when I tell him about Stanford's intentions. Matt's no stranger to guys being jerks to me and implying I'm cheap goods. But at my own request, he's never gotten violent with any of the guys who've treated me like I'm an ice cream sundae—something to consume, then move on to the next thing. I also have helped the situation by never dating any of his friends. That would have been way too weird.

"Are you ok?" he asks and glances off to the side.

"Who's with you?" I peer at the screen, as if narrowing my eyes would magically make me see who else is in the room. "It's not Mom, or Dad, or Joey, or Lizzy."

Matt shifts a little, and I can no longer see his face. Instead, he has the phone camera pressed up against the gray of his t-shirt. Annoyance flickers in my chest.

The phone shakes and his face comes back into view. "That's why I was calling, Brooke." He swallows. "I wanted to tell you that I—" He rubs his jaw. "I met someone."

My eyes widen, and my goopy paint hand flies to my open mouth without me telling it to do that. My brother, the perpetually single man who's famous for his two-date ultimatum, is telling *me* he met someone?

World? What is happening?

The paint gets in my mouth, and I gag at the acrylic taste before running to the sink. I rinse my mouth out and wash my hands, taking my time. I break up with a man, Matt finds someone. Life isn't fair.

Twins do things *together*. It's the whole point. Obviously we can't do everything together, but I don't like this. At all. The anxiety I corral into a neat pen in the far recesses of my mind escapes. I spend a moment forcing it back into its cage with deep breaths, but my fingers find my hair and start to tug on the roots, pulling out several of the long blonde strands. It's only when I see the pink one in my hand that I stop. *Get it together, Brooke.*

I paste on a fake smile and return to the phone call. "Is she with you right now?" I ask.

Matt leans back and adjusts the camera so that now I can see him sitting on the couch in his apartment as he wraps his arm around a beautiful brunette woman with her dark hair in a messy bun. She wears a bright blue sleeveless shirt that puts her impressively sculpted arms on display.

"Hi, I'm Melanie," she says, her voice soft and pleasant.

I do everything I can to push down the flare of jealousy that Matt is leaving me and finding love, and I'm not.

"Hi," is the only reply I can muster. I know I'm being unreasonable, but I'm still reeling from Stanford.

"Uh. Good talk, then," Matt interjects, teasing.

"Shut it," I snap in the unique twin language Matt and I created when we were toddlers. Not even our parents understand it, but we communicate perfectly in 'twin'.

"Are you guys, like, bilingual?" Melanie asks.

Matt gives me the *doom eyes*. He told her he had a twin, but he didn't tell her about our language. Oops, but also, what does he expect by dropping this bomb on me? There has *never* been a woman he wanted me to meet, let alone a woman snuggled up with him on his couch.

"Sorry, but I have to go. I have paint to mess up. Or wait, mess to paint up, or … I have to go. Bye."

I hang up the phone before I can say anything else stupid in front of Matt's *girlfriend* with the really great arms and really good hair.

I frown at the mess before setting my phone on the counter. Matt was supposed to be my support right now, and he's gone. I think for a moment about what to do, and I'm kneeling in the smears of paint when my phone rings again.

I throw my hands up, muttering, "I give up! Security deposit, you clearly don't want to come back to my bank account!"

I stomp to my phone, because I'm allowed dramatics at a time like this, and when I see it's Mom, I answer.

"Hi, honey," she says before tilting her head slightly and asking with serious blue eyes, "What's wrong?"

And at those words, I begin to cry, and cry, and cry. The anxiety escapes again, and I can't pen it by myself.

Mom says something to someone off the screen, and then I hear her say, "Hold on, I'll be over in a few minutes."

My parents live twenty minutes away from my apartment with my two younger siblings, Joey and Lizzy. Joey and Lizzy are not official twins, but they are of the Irish variety—both born in the same calendar year.

Apparently, my parents love having two babies at a time. Twins do that to you. Everything is better doubled. Except when one twin does something without the other. Like falling in love.

I'm slumped on the barstool at the kitchen counter when my mom knocks on my door before letting herself in with the emergency spare key she and my dad have.

"Honey," she says quietly, opening her arms, and I launch into them. My mother's hugs are the most powerful force in the world.

Words bubble out as I sink into her safety. "No one ever wants to try for me. Everyone I date just wants one thing, and I don't do that, and I just asked him to plan a date, and his plans were … not ok with me."

She rubs soothing circles on my back, and my breathing slows. Eventually the tears subside to quiet sniffles. She leads me to the couch, and I let her.

When she sits down next to me and angles her body so she's looking into my eyes, my heart is chafed and raw, but also loved. I'm grateful I have a relationship with my mom where I feel safe enough to be myself.

"Brookie. I think it might be a good time for you to go help Meemaw. You're done with college now, and I know you're working hard, but you can step away from your waitressing job. And I actually called earlier to ask if you would consider leaving the cafe, but now I think it's definitely a good idea."

I love my grandmother. I don't get to see her very often since she lives in West Virginia and I live in Marquette, Michigan.

"Meemaw?" I frown. "Is she ok?"

Mom sighs. "She broke her ankle and she'll be at a rehab facility after having surgery, but the truth is, she's getting older in age and values her independence. The problem is, we can't tell if she's losing her faculties and needs to be moved to a care home, or if she's just becoming more eccentric with her age."

"Even more eccentric?" I ask, visions of Meemaw doing ridiculous things over the years flipping through my mind. Mom nods, and her copper-colored hair shakes in the light. "What does she need?"

"Honestly, she needs someone to live with her. She's still very independent. You could work around there, just be there as her point of contact in case of emergencies. I think a change of scenery would do you some good."

I bite my lip. "Ok. But did you know Matt has a girlfriend?"

She nods.

"You knew!" I shriek. "You knew and you didn't tell me!"

"Matt called to tell me he met *the one* as soon as he saw her at the gym. He was worried about you taking the news poorly. He knows you haven't had the best luck with dating."

That's one way to put it.

"Ugh. Mom," I whine. Usually I don't whine, but I'm allowed to be dramatic right now. "Why does no one want to date me, like *date date* me?"

"It's because you haven't met the right one yet, sweetie." She stands and looks at the picture I was painting, perched on a three legged easel. It's a landscape of Lake Superior with a dark red sunset on the horizon. "You could sell these, you know."

I shrug. "It's just for me, Mom." Painting and crocheting keep my hands and mind busy, and that has always helped keep the trichotillomania at bay. The pink hair helps too. I don't want to pull out a strand that I spent money dyeing.

"That's fine, sweetie, but you have so much talent." She stoops down and picks up the supplies I left on the ground after the Leaning Tower of Easel incident. "Would you consider it?" she asks as she arranges the supplies neatly on my counter.

I know she isn't talking about selling my paintings. I close my eyes, and as I do, I see a vision of Matt and Melanie getting married and realize that Matt thinks this is *the one*. And I have nothing. As my mom kindly pointed out, I don't have anything that's really keeping me here. I mean, I have my family, but I'm a grown twenty-four-year-old woman. A change of scenery, a way out of the abysmal dating pool I've found myself drowning in … *I'll do it.*

When I open my eyes and nod at her, she claps her hands. "I'm so glad, Brooke. It will be good for you and Meemaw."

MEEMAW

Deep in the hills of West Virginia, a seventy-six-year-old woman limps along the hall of a post-surgical physical therapy rehabilitation center. She's stealthy—the benefit of her four-foot-eleven height and thin frame—and the only sound is the *swish-thump-swish* of her neon blue cast sliding along the linoleum floor.

Outside, the moon peeks in and out of cloud cover.

She hears a noise, the sound of one of the nurse's heavy footfalls.

She flattens herself against the wall, just feet from the exterior door to the parking lot. She holds her breath as she waits for the nurse to either turn down the other hallway or to find her.

Will she be given the freedom she craves?

Voices reach her ears.

"Have you seen June?" one nurse asks.

"No," another nurse answers. "Isn't she sleeping in her room?"

"Clearly you don't know June."

June sees her chance. She shuffles as quickly as she can to the exit door. She pushes it open, angling her thin, work-worn body through the crack.

She cackles as she stands on the sidewalk, tipping her face up to the cloud-covered moon.

And then the alarm sounds.

Frozen and unable to run with the cast on her foot, she puts her hands up as two nurses come running out of the same door she escaped from.

She lets out a frustrated curse as the nurses approach her.

She eyes the cars in the parking lot. Her car isn't here, but she knows how to hot-wire one. She watched videos one afternoon on YouTube.

It's not stealing if it's a matter of freedom.

"Miss June, I know you don't want to be here, but why are you running away in the middle of the night?" the younger of the two nurses asks. June likes him better. He has better manners than the older one.

She sniffs and assumes an air of dignity. "Can't a woman get some fresh air?"

"Not in the middle of the night. Your ankle isn't healed yet, Miss June."

"It's fine." An idea takes hold. "Call my grandson, Dr. Beckett Whistler. He'll tell you I'm fine to go home."

"Miss June, you never mentioned a grandson who was a doctor."

She lies and bobs her head, causing her silver hair to shake. "I forgot about him."

The nurses frown at each other.

"Do you have his phone number?" the male nurse asks.

"Of course I do."

She pulls out her phone and, with surprising deftness, locates his contact information. "Here." She shows them the phone. It reads: *Dr.*

Beckett Whistler (Next-door neighbor). "I will be leaving this place. And *he'll* tell you I can."

The nurses grimace. Clearly Dr. Beckett Whistler is not June's grandson. But she doesn't want to be here.

"Miss June," the younger nurse says placatingly. "We will call your surgeon in the morning. If your surgeon gives us the ok, you can go in the morning."

June harrumphs.

"Miss June," the older nurse says. "You know you can't walk on that cast, and you can't drive with it either."

June sniffs. The younger nurse extends an arm to her, and she leans on it, relieved to take some weight off the heavy cast on her foot.

The older nurse returns to the building and procures a wheel-chair. With as much dignity as she can muster, she sits down.

The young nurse takes over wheeling her back into the facility.

The alarms are still blaring from when June pushed open the emergency exit.

No one hears the deep voice crackling from June's cell phone.

"June? June? Is everything alright?"

2

DR. BECKETT WHISTLER

When I bought my house, I thought I'd be gaining peace and quiet after busy shifts in the E.R. It's idyllic, halfway up a mountain with a view of the New River below, and shares a drive with my neighbor. I did not anticipate my neighbor, a seventy-something-year-old woman, to be a source of constant annoyance.

Make no mistake, my dad taught me manners before he passed, and I will not be letting Miss June know how much her antics irritate me, but she is distinctly a thorn in my side.

Is it too much to ask for a neighbor who *doesn't* call me at two a.m. on my night off?

But she's also older, and she lives alone, and she tricked me into being her emergency contact when she brought me the absolute best fried chicken I'd ever eaten on the day I moved in. She's crafty.

As an E.R. doctor, I'm no stranger to long hours and late nights. In the next month, I'm finally transitioning to the day shift. Maybe then my sleep will become normal. For now, I'm awake.

I slide out of bed and throw on a pair of worn blue jeans, a black t-shirt, and a flannel shirt. I take a breath and run my hand through my short beard. I can't believe I'm doing this, but my conscience won't let me do anything else guilt-free. I'll never get any sleep if I don't.

I pull my phone from the charger and dial the number of Rejuvenate, the inpatient physical rehabilitation center June is staying at after her ankle surgery.

It's after hours, but someone should be at the desk. I follow the menu of options presented by the entirely too-chipper-for-the-middle-of-the-night recording. *Does no one realize no one wants to be in these places?*

By the time I'm connected to an actual human—because, of course, that's the last option and not the first—I'm already in my car and driving down the road.

"Hello, Rejuvenate In-Patient Physical Rehabilitation Center. This is the front desk. How can I help you?"

The woman's boredom grates on me. I grumble. *Must be nice. There's never been a boring night in the E.R.*

My voice comes out more gruff than I intended. That tends to be the way of things, if the nurses are to be believed, and the E.R. manager, and all my medical school evaluations…

I help people in emergencies. I have manners, I just don't have patience.

"I'm calling because June MacCord phoned me. Clearly there was an incident, and I need to check on her."

"Oh." There's murmured conversation on the other end of the line, and then, "Who is this?"

"Dr. Whistler. Miss MacCord's … emergency contact."

"Oh. Dr. Whistler. Sorry about that. Let me check with the charge nurse about Miss MacCord. Can I call you back?"

"No," I grumble. "I'm on my way."

"Oh. But it's late."

"Mmhmm."

"But…"

I hang up.

Twelve minutes and three hairpin mountain road turns later, I pull into the parking lot. I mutter a silent plea that June will be on her best behavior and everything will have been a mistake before killing the engine. Even as I hold out the tiny thread of hope that it was nothing more than an accidental pocket dial, I know it wasn't. There's always more to the story when June's involved.

Still, I've seen enough in my years of medicine to know that I need to check on her in person.

The door to the reception area slides open, and the woman at the front desk doesn't bother looking up. "Visiting hours are over," she says stiffly.

I fix her with a stern glare. "I'm Doctor Whistler. And I need to talk to the charge nurse and see Miss June MacCord before I leave."

"You're Doctor Whistler?" Her eyes rove over my body in appraisal. She leans forward, and I hate the not-so-subtle signals she's sending.

I force her gaze back to my face. "Yes." I'm curt. "The charge nurse, now."

She frowns before she steps away from the desk and through a door. I hear her, because she is clearly not trying to hide her words. "Dr. Whistler insists on seeing the charge nurse. And by the way, he'd be hot if he wasn't so … grumpy."

"Difficult patients, difficult doctors, is there anything beneath a charge nurse?"

"I'm not talking to him anymore. I mean if he'd apologize, I would go home with him in a heartbeat, but not with that attitude."

I roll my eyes. The desperation of this woman is something I would not touch while wearing a hazmat suit.

A half moment later, the charge nurse walks behind the desk. She's probably close to forty, and has the look of someone who's worn out from how taxing her job is.

"Dr. Whistler?"

I cross my arms over my chest and nod.

"Can I see some ID?"

I hand over my license and hospital ID.

She holds a blue file folder in her left hand and flips it open. "You are Miss MacCord's…"

"Emergency contact."

"Right." The charge nurse quirks a brow at me. "And you're here because…?"

"Miss MacCord called me half an hour ago. It's unusual to receive a phone call from a person in the middle of the night when they're in an in-patient facility after surgery."

"Well…" The charge nurse grimaces. "There was a small incident with Miss MacCord and two of our nurses not that long ago."

"An incident?" My eyes narrow. "What kind of incident? Did she reinjure her ankle? Her surgery was less than forty-eight hours ago."

The charge nurse levels me with a stern glare. "Miss MacCord does not want to be here. She attempted to leave the facility by way of an emergency exit. She was found before she caused any damage to her ankle or the facility."

"I'd like to see her."

"She's asleep. Visiting hours are over."

I stare her down.

"Fine." She sighs. "Just not long. She's in Room 63."

She buzzes me back into the facility, and I pass by the desk, keeping my eyes on the hall in front of me and definitely not turning back to the receptionist with the wandering eyes and suggestive—and unwelcome—invitation.

I follow the numbers down the linoleum hallway with the scuffed walls and dents common in medical facilities where people can't walk without equipment as they recover from surgeries. At Room 63, I stop and knock once. I open the door quietly, in case she's asleep.

She's not.

Just my luck.

"Beckett!" she exclaims, clapping her hands. "I knew you'd come and get me."

Her words hit me with the force of a truck. I reel back. "Get you?"

"That's why you're here. I called, and you came to get me." She drops her voice to a conspiratorial whisper. "This place is unAmerican."

I rein in a snort. "UnAmerican?"

"They do not uphold the Constitution. Freedom, liberty, and justice for *all.* They're restricting my rights to freedom."

"Miss June." I bite down on my teeth so hard that I'm speaking through a clenched jaw, but I have to say something. "Do you realize you just had surgery less than two days ago?"

She shakes her head. "Of course I realize that. I am completely all there." She taps her head with her knuckles as she speaks. "Now take me home, young man."

I turn to find the charge nurse and two other male nurses standing in the hallway, smirking at our conversation. *This is what I get for leaving the door open.*

"Pull out her release paperwork," I say. "I'll supervise her in her own home recovery and connect with the surgeon."

"That's my grandson," June says with pride.

I spin on my heel. "I'm not your grandson. I'm your emergency contact and neighbor."

She shrugs. "Taters and onions go together."

The nurses snort behind me.

The charge nurse hands me June MacCord's file, along with a stack of *Against Medical Advice* release papers.

It's thirty more minutes before I'm wheeling June out to my old truck.

"Dabnabit," she says when she sees me pull the key out of my pocket.

"What?"

"I was hoping to hot-wire a car to get out of here."

I scrub a hand down my face, letting my fingers tug slightly on my beard.

This woman is going to be the death of me.

3

BROOKE

Lizzy and Joey are high school freshmen, and both earned their varsity letters this year in cross country. I thought I'd have a week or two to get my things together, and that Mom would make the trip with me, but instead, a four a.m. phone call from Meemaw changed the plans.

"Brooke, she needs someone right now," Mom begged. And because I already committed to going and staying with her through her recovery period for at least the next two months, I'm shooed on my way.

Lizzy and Joey's varsity letters mean that Mom couldn't miss their big race this weekend. So instead of Mom and I going on a road trip, Matt is driving with me down to West Virginia. I'll have Meemaw's ancient car to drive while I'm there, and Matt will return to Michigan and his girlfriend without me.

"What has you all quiet?" Matt's voice jars me from thoughts about his girlfriend, who I just don't really like.

I roll my eyes, then focus on the road.

Matt tries again, this time in *twin*. "It's about Melanie, isn't it?"

"No," I snap, faster than I should have—and now he definitely knows he's on the right track.

"Brooke, you just haven't met the right person yet. Maybe you will when you're here."

I let out a snort before adopting a dramatic, fake Southern accent. "So many handsome men in these here hills. Just the right kind of man to challenge me to adventure and *not* want what I'm not giving."

Matt snorts. "Can we stop at the rest area?"

"Being a passenger princess too much for you?"

"Hardly. I let you drive my car because I know you like to be in charge. Maybe it's time to let go a little bit."

Great. Now my brother is calling out my insecurities.

"Fine," I huff. "There's a rest stop in two miles. But I'm only stopping because I need to go."

"And I'm driving the rest of the way."

"What? No, I'm not ready for that."

"Brooke, let go a little."

I snarl at the road in front of me, but a yawn escapes me, and I think, *Maybe it wouldn't be so bad if I got to sit in the front seat and nap.*

Carly Rae Jepson's "Friday" wakes me. It *is* Friday, and Matt has always loved that song, but the fact that he turned it up to the highest possible volume means that I jump in my seat, whack my head against the window, and scream.

"Matt!" I shriek. "Why would you do that? You gave me a heart attack!"

Matt sits in the driver's seat of his truck, arms crossed, and a smug grin on his face. He tips his head toward my window and raises his brows. The music still blares. I turn my head and discover a man standing just at the place where the driveway splits to a different house. My eyes widen at his very attractive physique. He's wearing a short sleeve black tee, and his forearms are crossed over his chest, which makes them flex. He's not the tallest man—maybe only five-foot-ten or so—but he's taller than my own short five-foot-three stature. I can't see his eyes behind the sunglasses he wears, but he has coppery hair, and a short reddish beard covers his jaw. He holds a bunch of letters and scowls at me.

To my mortification, there is very clearly drool on the window.

I open the door, which thankfully stops the music, and climb out of the truck. I reach into the back and grab hold of my duffle bag. It's heavy. Matt has already disappeared inside Meemaw's house.

Would it be nice if Matt helped me? Yes. Do I expect him to do it without me directing him? No.

I sigh because my brother has learned nothing. *Good luck with Melanie, you twerp!*

I loop the strap across my chest to distribute the weight better, then pull a moving box out of the truck bed and balance that on my hip. There's a pair of hiking boots and hot-pink high heels that I tossed into the bed right before we left that need to come inside too. Grunting, I reach into the truck and pull each shoe toward me. There's one more box and my backpack left. But I am not making more trips than I have to.

I can get this all inside in one go.

I place the box on the ground, slip off the duffle, and crawl across the blue-painted truck bed, where I reach the box that slid into the farthest corner during the drive. When I'm back on solid ground, I stare for a moment at the pile of belongings that will make up my life for the next three months.

It takes a moment, but I figure out how to carry it all. I am nothing if not efficient. I am strong, I don't need Matt's help—besides, I can do it on my own.

I loop the duffle strap across my body, which causes the bag to hang awkwardly by my knees, then the backpack with my crochet supplies and journal, then the stack of two boxes with the shoes on top. I can hardly see in front of me, but it's fine.

These boxes are heavy. But I'm strong. I will not be defeated.

With each step up the sharply graded driveway, the load becomes harder to manage, but I eventually make it to the side door of Meemaw's house.

Matt stands just inside and swings the door open for me.

Sweat runs down my face as I shove past him. I don't see the edge of the step up into the kitchen and whack my shin on it.

Howling in pain, I yelp and fly forward. Thankfully, it's only one step, so the boxes land on the floor and skitter away. Clutching my shin, I turn to Matt to yell at him about his lack of manners and how he should have helped me. I'm just in time to see Matt lift his hand in a wave and offer the man from the other driveway a cheeky grin.

From where I sit, my hand massaging the pain shooting down my shin, I can see the man as he stomps away.

"Looks like a real friendly neighbor you've got here, Brookie." Matt closes the door.

I sigh. The man would be attractive, but he didn't help me either. *Oh well.*

I reach out my foot and kick Matt's calf.

4

DR. BECKETT WHISTLER

June MacCord's granddaughter from Michigan, of all places, is coming to stay with her. Really? Her family is sending a grandkid to keep an eye on this woman whose greatest desire in life is to hot-wire a car. *A grandkid.* What on earth are they thinking? Now I'll have to babysit both June *and* the kid.

In a bad mood, I stomp to the mailboxes at the bottom of the steep driveway. Just as I reach where the driveways split, a bright blue Ford Ranger pickup pulls in and parks. Instead of opening the door, the driver turns the volume all the way up. I am concerned for my own eardrums, but then a woman gets out of the passenger seat, and now I'm worried about my eyes. Granddaughter this may be, grandKID this is not.

She's short and petite, and her blonde hair is pulled up in a ponytail with streaks of pink running through it. She's wearing black stretchy pants that stop just before the shin and a hot pink short sleeve shirt. I am entranced by her graceful movements as she strides to the back of the truck.

The man has already stalked inside. He's taller than her, and clearly muscular, with the kind of gym muscles that only come from an insane amount of protein and intense workouts. Annoyance that he left without so much as asking if she needed help carrying her things makes my frown deepen.

I scowl at the door to Miss June's house, where the man disappeared. Dad's lectures about manners around a lady unlock my frozen body, and just as I'm about to call to the woman and ask if she needs help, she begins carrying a veritable Leaning Tower of Pisa up the driveway. She buckles a little under the load but keeps going.

Who is this tiny woman? And how is she so strong?

I watch in fascination, again frozen, but this time in admiration, as her legs carry her up the steep slope.

The side door of June's house swings open, and I see the man watching me. His bemused expression tells me that he misinterpreted my admiration of the way the woman's legs chugged up the driveway as appreciation for her glutes.

Fine. Just because being friendly is hard for me doesn't mean I have lost all sense of manners. I didn't stare. I just noticed her attractiveness and moved on.

Anger rears its head as I think about this woman—who is clearly too good for this man—carrying her things up the driveway. *Is basic chivalry dead?* I certainly did nothing to resuscitate it just now, but really, what kind of a deadbeat boyfriend is this guy?

My throat cords as the man in the doorway waves at me.

What if he's her husband?

I shake my head to clear the thought just in time to hear the woman yell 'HEY' and crumple down. The door swings closed.

Stupid Hippocratic Oath.

She fell. She could be injured. It's not my property. I'm not on duty. But I swore I'd do no harm. I swore that I'd help.

I tuck the envelopes—bills, of course—into my back jeans pocket and stride over to June's and knock on the side door.

The granddaughter opens it. "Can I help you?" she asks. I get a good look at her blue eyes, thick lashes, and pink lips.

I raise my sunglasses and perch them on my head. "Yeah, uh, is everything ok? Did anyone get hurt?"

She laughs. "No." Then she sticks out a hand. "Hi, I'm Brooke. I'm staying with my Meemaw for a while so she can heal up."

A screeching noise hits my eardrums. "Who's there, Brooke?" June yells from somewhere within the house.

Brooke studies me while I stare at her and try not to notice how very pretty she is, or the small scar to the left of her eye. Stitches that didn't heal quite right.

She jolts me back to reality when she says, "Uh … ok. I don't know what to tell her. Who are you?" Her hand is no longer extended, and I'm an idiot.

Annoyed at myself now, I answer, but my mouth is dry, and my upper lip sticks to my front teeth. I must look exactly like Beast interacting with Belle. Thinking of *Beauty and the Beast* makes me think of Addie, and thinking of Addie always brings out the worst in me. It's not a total surprise to me that when the words come, they are biting. "Dr. Beckett Whistler."

She rolls her eyes at my pretentiousness.

Who really introduces themselves so formally when we're neighbors? I am the opposite of a friendly neighbor.

"Brooke?" June calls again. "Who's there?"

My eyes are malfunctioning because I'm not telling them to stare at her, but they're locked on her pretty face, and when she hollers back, "No one, Meemaw!" and slams the door, I know I royally messed up.

I tromp back to my house, letting thoughts of Addie flood my brain. I haven't felt anything for a woman in a very long time, but I felt *something* just then. I don't like it.

My phone buzzes in my back jeans pocket, and I pull it out. It's my best friend, Ben. "Hey," I say into the phone.

"Hey, a couple of us are going hiking. You should come."

"Yeah. When and where?"

"Logan met a tourist … so Endless Wall at six."

"He didn't want to take her to Nuttleberg? Better places to make out along that trail," I quip. Logan is definitely a ladies' man, and he certainly uses his charms on the tourists.

Ben's laugh is mirthless. "C'mon, Beck. You can't fault him for looking for love—"

"Yeah, well, I found it already, and we know what happened there."

"Ok. Beck is blue, we get it. You've been blue for what, four years now? It's time to get back out there, man."

"You try it first." It's a low blow, and I know it, but I don't care. Telling me to get over Addie is like telling Ben to get over his first motorcycle. It's a rust bucket on two wheels, but he won't give it up.

"I'm going to let that one go, but are you coming to Endless Wall?"

I take a breath, hold it, count to three, and blow it out again. "Fine, but if Logan gets too handsy, I'm out."

"We know," Ben retorts before hanging up.

5

BROOKE

"Let me see you, Brookie," Meemaw demands after I slam the door on Dr. Beckett Whistler. What a pretentious jerk. It's too bad, because he's incredibly attractive. Chocolate brown eyes, short red beard, strong, chiseled jaw, muscular arms that aren't as jacked as Matt's—but he has the personality of an ogre.

"Coming, Meemaw." I let my shoulders slump. Dr. Beckett Whistler definitely was checking me out as I stood there, but he's a jerk. So, that flare of attraction I felt at first, it just can't be anything. *How disappointing—again.*

I make my way through Meemaw's kitchen to her living room, where Matt sits with her on a faded floral couch. Meemaw's foot is elevated on a footstool, and the ancient rabbit ear antenna TV is on. It's playing a black-and-white episode of "The Beverly Hillbillies" because there's Granny Clampett doing something questionable.

I force a smile as I join Meemaw on the other side of the couch. "Brookie Cookie." Meemaw's eyes flash with worry. "Sit." She looks at the TV. "Wish I could find me some Texas tea."

I sit and she turns her beady blue eyes to me.

"What's wrong, gal?"

Matt snorts, but my glare over the top of Meemaw's head turns it into a cough real quick.

"Nothing's wrong, Meemaw."

"Sure, honey. And you aren't mad or upset, sure as idiots don't ask dumb questions."

I shake my head, trying to follow her train of thought, but failing.

"I'm tired from the drive, Meemaw," I deflect, but I can't tell her about Matt and Melanie with Matt sitting right there. And I don't really want to tell her about Dr. Beckett Whistler either.

Meemaw leans into me and gives me a hug, and her familiar scent of butterscotch and moonshine, with a hint of lard, fills my senses.

"When do you have to leave, Matt?" Meemaw asks.

"Soon, Meemaw. Sorry I can't stay long, but I have to get back."

"You can't leave till tomorrow," Meemaw announces imperiously as she straightens. "I need you to help me around here. Such a strapping young man. Your muscles are enormous. Did you pay for those with that plastic surgery?"

I bite my lip to keep from laughing. Matt scowls at me over Meemaw's head.

"No, Meemaw, these are *not* from plastic surgery. I own a gym now."

"That's so nice you're a gym teacher. Those kids with ADHD need that movement. I hear the dyes are to blame. But how will I be able to wear bright red if they ban all the dyes?"

Matt's eyes widen. Meemaw has always been eccentric, but is this willful misunderstanding of information, or is she confused? Our Meemaw decoding skills are a little rusty. "Uh. Well, the dyes are food dyes."

"What has this world come to? People are dyeing their food now?"

"Uh … yeah."

Meemaw snorts. "In my day, it was enough to just serve it to a man, not try to entice him by making it look pretty." She pats Matt's arm. "You men need to stop being so high-maintenance."

Matt's eyes meet mine across Meemaw's head. As a personal trainer and gym owner, he is particular about his food, and this conversation has spiraled out of his control.

Meemaw springs up as best she is able to with her foot in the cast. "Bring me my scooter, Matthew."

Matt wheels a knee scooter over to Meemaw, and she slips onto it with surprising deftness. "All this talk of food has made me hungry," she declares. "You'll be wanting fried chicken?"

Matt grins. "Definitely, Meemaw. No one makes it like you."

I have it on good authority that Matt won't touch fried chicken unless it's Meemaw's.

He grins as he catches my not-so-subtle eye roll. "How can we help?"

"You"—she scoots past him into the kitchen—"can stay out of my kitchen, but Brooke needs to come. A woman needs to know how to make a man-pleasin' dish."

Matt holds back a laugh. "Welcome to the eighteenth century, Brooke," he whispers as I pass him.

I use my small stature to swing my elbow into the soft spot just above his hip. He doubles over, but he's still shaking with unreleased mirth.

If I can count on one thing, it's that I never know what Meemaw will do next. And that the next few months of me living here and helping out will be … interesting.

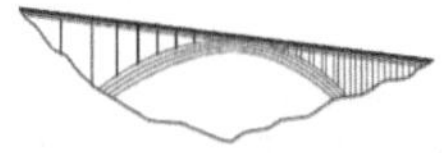

We're all up early the next morning. Meemaw, because she's always up before the sun, and Matt, because he needs to head back to Michigan and Melanie. I heard him talking to her on the phone last night, and I wanted to gag. If I could have, I would have grabbed the phone through the wall and yelled, *"That's my brother you're talking to!"*

Unfortunately, the wall separating us is not soundproof, but it did prevent me from phasing through and throwing his phone into the nearest river.

At least he had to sleep on the lumpy pull-out couch while I got the guest bedroom. It's a tiny pink square with a twin bed, and Meemaw's craft supplies crammed into every nook and cranny, but it wasn't the back-breaking sofa.

Meemaw can't get down the steps to the driveway, so she says her goodbyes from the kitchen. She whispers something into Matt's ear, and he flushes while he shakes his head. She leans in again, and both of them look directly at me. Matt grins and winks before pulling Meemaw into a hug and placing a kiss on her wrinkled cheek.

"Take care of Meemaw, Brooke," he says as we walk down the porch steps and over to his truck. "She's a schemer, but I think you'll have some fun if you go along with it."

"Drive safe?" I ask, in twin.

"Of course," he says back.

I swallow a lump in my throat. I have to say something about Melanie, about how he shouldn't move too fast with her, but just as I open my mouth to warn him, an old, white, scuffed-up Toyota pickup truck barrels up the driveway, blaring loud music.

Dr. Beckett Whistler—again.

The windows are rolled down, and I catch a glimpse of his face. He looks haggard, sleep-deprived. He parks in the adjoining drive-way and climbs out of his truck, turning to face us with his arms crossed over his chest.

Matt waves at him, but Dr. Beckett Whistler scowls.

Matt looks at me and grins. "That guy"—he tips his head toward the doctor—"is the one for you."

I roll my eyes up to heaven and back. "Matt, just because you found someone doesn't mean I ever will."

"Hey." He tips my chin up so I'm looking at him. "You are the biggest pain I know, and you need someone who is an equal level of obnoxious for you. That guy"—he jerks his thumb over his shoulder—"he's got it."

"Whatever, Mattie."

He opens his arms, and I step into his hug. We joke and tease and are often physical with our antics, but the truth is, we need each other. We're twins, and it's hard when we're apart. A lot of people don't understand it because they don't have a twin, but Matt is a piece of me.

Tears beckon when I straighten.

Matt smirks before climbing into the driver's seat. "Go make friends. I've got a good feeling about him." He shoots a finger gun directly at Dr. Beckett Whistler before putting the truck in reverse.

I stand there after Matt leaves, watching Dr. Whistler stare at his retreating blue truck with a frown.

Matt couldn't be more wrong.

MEEMAW

Nothing could be more frustrating to the septuagenarian of 6363 Mountain Hideaway Road than a lack of freedom. And nothing could stop her from accessing the emergency chocolate chip cookie ingredients stashed in the cabinet on top of her refrigerator. Chocolate chip cookies *must* be made, and they must be made now.

Never mind the granddaughter sleeping in the spare room. Never mind that it's two a.m., and never mind that, at her four-foot-eleven height, she cannot reach the cabinet without standing on something.

She uses the knee scooter her neighbor brought over after rescuing her from the prison of the rehab center to line up with the edge of the fridge.

Shrewd eyes size up the opponent. A lesser woman would be deterred, but not June MacCord. She is hard-working, and her brain is filled with ingenuity.

After a moment's consideration, she knows what to do. She swings her lithe body sideways, gripping the edge of the fridge, and places both knees on the scooter seat. Using her bony fingers and the crack of the fridge seal, she pulls herself up to standing on her good foot.

Her eyes peer over the top of the fridge. It's dusty in that space between the appliance and the cabinet, but even dust can't deter her from her mission. She arches her body closer, shifting to her tiptoes.

Her fingers find purchase on the cabinet knobs, and she swings the door open. The movement jars the scooter away. It's enough to cause her to lose her balance. Her hands grasp the bag of flour, the bag of white sugar, the brown sugar, as she scrambles for something to stabilize her. It's not enough. Her fingers close on a bag of chocolate chips as the scooter rolls farther away, and June MacCord falls backward.

In the chaos that ensues, chocolate chips scatter all over the kitchen floor, and June lets loose a string of swear words that would make a sailor blush.

Her granddaughter, wearing hot-pink pajamas, hears the crash and comes running.

June lies on the floor, conscious but in pain.

With nothing else to be done for June, the granddaughter calls 9-1-1.

6

DR. BECKETT WHISTLER

It's been the world's longest shift in the E.R. Car accidents, stitches, a broken leg, and a case of norovirus with severe dehydration have kept all of us at the small regional hospital busy. My shift begins at 6 p.m. and ends at 6 a.m. It's 2:30 in the morning, and I am just now eating my lunch.

"Dr. Whistler?" Peony, the charge nurse, walks into the small room just as I'm about to take a bite of my sub sandwich. I've worked with Peony for a while. She's close to my age, twenty-seven or twenty-eight. Most importantly, she's quiet, but competent. She doesn't annoy me the way most of the newer nurses do. "We need you immediately. There's an older woman who fell."

I sigh and put the sandwich back in its wrapper, then toss it in the tiny fridge. "What do I need to know?"

"She's a frequent flyer here, so I think you two have met." Peony says it drily, and I'm immediately concerned about *which* one of our accident-prone E.R. regulars now requires my attention.

Peony hands me a folder with a chart. I flip the file open.

June MacCord.

Immediately, a swoop of alarm hits my stomach. "What's wrong with her?"

"She fell. She seems cognizant, and isn't in too much pain on her injured foot, but we're concerned about an injury to the other ankle. She's definitely got some swelling. Said she had a hankering for cookies and fell off her scooter."

I scrub a hand down my beard, tugging on it with irritation. *Cookies? At two in the morning? And how did she fall off the scooter? I brought it over for her so that she* wouldn't *fall.* It was supposed to be June-proof.

"What room is she in?" I grit out through clenched teeth.

"Seventeen." She starts to walk away, but calls over her shoulder, "Good luck, Doctor."

I'm tired. I'm hungry. And now I have to deal with June. Will my neighbor ever cease being a source of annoyance?

My footsteps are heavy as I paste on what I hope is a passably professional face. I knock twice on the heavy wood door before opening it. My eyes take in the room, and everything stops.

June MacCord sits on a hospital bed, a warm blanket across her lap and her feet elevated. Standing next to her, staring at me, is June MacCord's granddaughter. I haven't seen her since early yesterday when I creeped on her and her boyfriend's goodbye. She doesn't wear wedding rings, so the guy isn't her spouse—yet. Their goodbye was weird. It was a long hug, and I swore I would leave when they started kissing, but they never did. She was not dressed then as she is now, but I was still distracted by her. She's pretty.

And now she's here. In front of me. Wearing bright pink pajamas with a button-up shirt and matching pink shorts.

Our gazes lock. I am frozen. I cannot move. *Why is this woman here in my E.R. and dressed like this? Why do I like it so much?*

June cackles. "I knew you'd take care of me!"

The granddaughter scowls at me, and I turn my attention to June. She is my patient, even if the toned arms and hint of legs on her granddaughter are distracting.

"June," I grumble. "What now?"

"Well, do you want the long story or the short version?"

"Which one will help me know what we need to do to get you back home and out of my hair?" I quip.

The granddaughter opens her mouth as she watches my exchange with June. She might be about to speak, but June butts in.

"That would be the long story." She pats her granddaughter's hand. "But first, would you get Brookie Cookie here a chair? She insists she won't sit until I've been seen by a doctor."

Brookie Cookie? I hope against hope that this is a nickname, and that the attractive woman who is currently my neighbor wasn't born to insane parents who love rhymes. But June is her grandmother, so absolutely nothing is off the table. And wait, didn't June say something about cookies being the reason she's here? Does *Brooke* have anything to do with this?

I turn and grab the chair from beside the door.

"He's very attractive, don't you think, Brookie?" June whispers loudly enough that everyone knows I heard her.

I take a moment before turning around and pretend I didn't just hear a seventy-six-year-old woman ogle me.

When I place the chair by June, I catch a glimpse of Brooke's face. It's mottled red.

June pats the chair. "Come on. Sit down, Brooke, and then I can tell Doc here all about what happened."

Brooke shuffles around the bed and sits in the chair, her eyes on anything but me. I, however, cannot look away from her legs—they're tan and muscular and end in fluffy pink slippers.

"It all started when I was watching that baking show Brooke likes," June starts, breaking my leg-induced trance.

I look at Brooke, fixing her with a stern glare. She should know better.

Brooke's eyes widen, and she opens her mouth, then shuts it again.

"Yep." June nods. "She left it in the DVCR. The one on Netflix about cake that looks like real things."

"Meemaw," Brooke interjects. "You're making it sound like this is *my* fault."

"Who said that? Because I didn't."

Brooke's cheeks flush, and she stares me directly in the eye. There's a fire there. It's intriguing. "I can assure you that I was *not* intending for this to happen. I watched an episode of *Is it Cake?* and went to bed. I didn't think I'd need to log out of Netflix to prevent a problem."

Ok, she has a point. This really isn't her fault.

"Then what?" I ask gruffly.

June pats Brooke's hand again. "Then I decided I needed to have a treat and teach those hooligans a lesson."

What hooligans? And what lesson?

"At two in the morning?" I inquire.

June's blue eyes pin me with their glare. "If those young people can bake such ridiculous contraptions, surely my cookies are worth a prize. I was going to bake them and mail them to the show. Teach those hotshot bakers that real food doesn't need to masquerade as something else. It can just be food. Your generation is so full of over-complicating everything. It's like when people slide into DMs on that internet business. Either you're sleeping together or you're not."

Brooke's hand flies to her mouth. I cram my eyes shut at June's bluntness.

"Ok, then." I blow out a breath. "I'm still not sure how you fell off your scooter."

"Oh, well, I couldn't reach the ingredients, so I stood on it."

"You stood on the scooter? The scooter that rolls? You *stood* on it?"

"Well, I couldn't very well get a stool to stand on with this ball and chain." June gestures to her cast-clad foot.

"Yeah, and common sense is a flower that doesn't grow in every-one's garden," I retort, but regret it immediately when Brooke's blue eyes snap to mine in indignation at my tone.

June cackles. "Your meemaw taught you that?"

I shrug before I drag my eyes away from the challenge in Brooke's. "Let's take a look at what we're dealing with."

I gesture to June's legs while sliding gloves over my hands.

"Swollen," I announce as I run my hands over her ankle. "Are you in pain?"

"Not really. It hurt like the dickens at first, but I drank some moon-shine before the ambulance people took me away from my home."

I scowl as I glare at Brooke. "You let her drink moonshine?"

"I stopped her as soon as I could, but it wasn't easy to pry the bottle away."

"Yeah, well, now we don't totally know what we're dealing with, so that's not helpful at all."

Brooke's fists clench at the sides of her pajama shorts, drawing my attention back to her legs. She stands up, and I'm amazed at her tiny stature but giant personality. "I don't think it's your *job*, Doctor Beckett Whistler, to tell *me* that I'm not enough. It *is* your job, Doc-tor Beckett Whistler, to help my grandmother get better. Do no harm—the Hippocratic Oath. Any of those ring a bell?"

My hand is on June's shin, but my mind is backfiring. Brooke said my full name. And I really liked how it sounded coming from her lips. I didn't like the anger directed at me behind her voice, but my sarcasm and poor people skills make it my own fault.

June coughs, and I move my hand. "I'm ordering X-rays. They'll wheel you back in a bit. I don't think you've broken your non-surgically repaired ankle, but we need to be sure. You can follow up with your surgeon tomorrow if the X-ray shows anything. Good night, Miss June."

I escape the room before either of them can say anything else.

Peony stops me in the hall, where I lean against the wall. I'm breathing hard and heavy after that because it's the middle of the night and my cortisol just skyrocketed. And, also Brooke. I can't get her out of my mind.

"Dr. Whistler?" Peony asks, leaning on the handles of an empty wheelchair. "You alright?"

I let out a heavy sigh. "Yeah. Miss June's my neighbor. And she's … a lot."

Peony laughs, and the sound is nice. I study her face for a moment. She's pretty enough, with long brown hair, deep brown eyes, and a smile that quirks up on one side, but when I look at her, nothing is there. No flare of attraction, no desire to interact with her on more than a professional level.

"That's one way to put it," Peony replies before opening the door to June MacCord's room and bringing the wheelchair inside.

I watch as she sashays around me, her strides athletic and long, and her movements graceful. And it does *nothing*. Objectively, Peony is attractive. But I have no interest. I was hoping that my interactions with June MacCord's granddaughter were a fluke. That my brain and body are just experiencing biological urges after four years of nothing.

The fact that I feel attraction around Brooke and no one else is very, very bad news.

7

BROOKE

Meemaw. Is. On. My. List.

The woman is treating the hospital staff like she's royalty, and they're letting her get away with it? Does no one understand that this woman is crazy? Being Meemaw's favorite granddaughter is fun. Being Meemaw's emergency contact and caretaker is *not*.

I scrub my hand along the tension in my cheekbones and jaw, trying not to scream.

Meemaw just asked the nurse for extra-hot blankets, and also a mason jar of moonshine since 'that Dr. Whistler with the nice behind didn't give her any pain meds.' The reason he didn't give her any pain meds *is* that she drank moonshine before coming to the hospital, and we don't know how much. She certainly won't admit it.

In the meantime, she's ready to be discharged with nothing more than a scare, a light sprain on her previously good ankle, and apparently no common sense.

The nurse with the pretty brown hair and the brown eyes that look like she can see into your soul comes into the room. "Miss Mac-Cord, I have your discharge papers." She turns to me. "I can tell you're ready to get out of here."

She doesn't say it unkindly, but it's 6:45 a.m., I'm still in my pajamas, hospital rooms are cold, I'm tired, I've been here all night, and who knows what mischief Meemaw's going to get up to now. I did *not* realize that being at Meemaw's meant I had to watch her every move, including in the middle of the night. So yes, I'm ready to get out of here.

"Yeah," I snap. "Isn't everyone?"

Peony arches one perfectly shaped brow before turning back to Meemaw. "Miss MacCord, you will have to be very careful for the next few days as the swelling goes down. You can wear a walking boot or a very supportive shoe to walk around your house, but you cannot leave your house. No more baking in the middle of the night. If you need something, please ask your granddaughter." Peony lowers her voice and stage whispers, "She doesn't want to be here, you know."

Meemaw studies me. "You're right. Brookie Cookie doesn't want to be here. I'll just take those papers and be on my way then." She sits up on the bed, moving like she expects to hop off it.

"You'll have to be wheeled out."

Meemaw scowls.

"You can drive her home, Brooke? Miss MacCord should not do any driving until she's cleared by her surgeon."

"Yeah," I say, exhaustion lacing my words. "I can drive."

"Great, then just sign here saying that you received discharge papers, and then you're good to go."

Peony takes the papers and disappears, reappearing with a wheelchair just a moment later.

The lights are hazy, and everything has a fuzzy glow around it as Peony rolls a chipper Meemaw to the front of the hospital, and I shuffle in oversized pink slippers down the halls.

We reach the front of the hospital, and Peony calls over her shoulder, "Should I stay with Miss MacCord while you bring your vehicle around?"

My eyes blink in the strange light. Everything wobbles. *What vehicle? We came in the ambulance.* I stare at Peony's face. *How did she get her eyebrows shaped like that?*

"Brooke?" A deep voice interrupts my eyebrow-induced jealousy, and I turn my head toward the sound. It's Dr. Beckett Whistler.

I feel the frown forming on my face, but then the floor is coming closer, and I can't figure out why.

Strong arms steady me, and I'm instantly warmer.

"Peony? What's going on?"

"Miss MacCord has been discharged, and I suggested we wait here while Brooke brings the vehicle around, but I don't think Brooke is used to all-nighters. Clearly, she shouldn't drive."

I'm leaning against the warmth of the man holding me. I have a sense of the conversation happening about me, but I don't care. I let my eyes close as I lean into solid warmth. The warmth sighs.

"I happen to live next door to Miss MacCord. I'll bring my truck around and take the two of them home."

"Do you think she's ok?"

My eyes are still closed, but I sense the perusal of my face and flutter one eye open.

He laughs, and I'm surprised by the richness of the sound. It's like turtle cheesecake, or even better—double chocolate cheesecake with peanut butter.

"She's fine. She's just tired."

Meemaw says something under her breath, but I don't catch it. I do catch Peony's sharp intake of breath and her "Miss MacCord!" which tells me whatever Meemaw said was wildly inappropriate, but I'm too tired to care.

Dr. Whistler leads me to a bench and presses my shoulder until I sit on it. "Stay here, Brooke, ok? I'll drive you and June home."

"Ok. You sound like cheesecake."

The low rumble of a laugh hits my ears, and I like the sound. I lean my head back against the wall and close my eyes.

8

DR. BECKETT

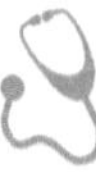

My old truck has served me well, and I've never felt a pang of embarrassment about being a doctor who drives something most people would consider a beater—until this moment.

I pull the truck into the circle drive by the main doors and do a quick scan of the floor. There's only one receipt from the grocery store languishing on the mat. I scoop it up and shove it into my scrubs pocket. I don't know why I care, but suddenly I really want Brooke to like being in my truck.

That thought stops me cold.

No. No, Beck. You don't do this. Remember, you got burned so bad last time you cared you needed an emotional heart transplant.

I hop out of the truck, roll my shoulders a few times, and then walk through the hospital doors. Peony is chatting with June, and Brooke is … snoring softly.

It's not that much, but she's asleep, and her head lolls to the side. Her pink pajamas match the pink in her hair cascading over her shoulder.

My mouth goes dry.

June cackles. "If you're interested, I give you my blessing."

My eyes snap to June, whose eyes sparkle. Peony's slightly raised eyebrows are even more concerning.

"I think I shouldn't be the one to wake her up," I say, trying to play it off like I was staring at Brooke because I couldn't figure out how to wake her up, not because she's so beautiful it hurts my heart.

"I can wake her, Dr. Whistler," Peony replies with a tight-lipped smile. "You get Miss June in the car."

I give a curt nod, because that's all I can manage under Peony's scrutiny, and take over wheeling June out to my truck. June reaches a hand behind her and rests it on my own. "You know, Brooke needs a strong man. I worry about her. Men these days are just not what they used to be. I know she wouldn't be here if it wasn't for her dating troubles."

"Dating troubles?" The question flies out of my mouth before I can stop it.

June hums in response. "Yes, her mother told me all about it. A string of bad boyfriends. Thank goodness she broke it off with the last one."

June's words somersault through my mind, but we've reached the truck. "I'm going to pick you up and help you into the back bench. You can ride with your feet elevated that way."

I hate that I'm instructing her to ride improperly as an E.R. doctor, but there's no way she can sit comfortably with her cast in the tiny space behind the front seats.

I help June into the cab, and when she smiles at me, I'm filled with an odd sense of gratitude for the eccentric woman who is my neighbor and *had* to bake cookies in the middle of the night and bring her granddaughter with her to the E.R. It doesn't hurt that June just told me her granddaughter is single.

I turn and watch Peony walk with Brooke to my truck. The two women are similar in height and stature, but my eyes are drawn to Brooke. Pink pajamas and fuzzy slippers do not do great things for my pulse.

"Take care, Brooke," Peony says as she grabs the wheelchair handles and takes it back into the hospital.

"Thanks, Peony," Brooke replies before meeting my gaze. She shifts uncomfortably and looks at the ground. "Thanks for giving us a ride home. We came in the ambulance."

In a normal world, where Beck Whistler is functioning as a normal human being and not someone whose fiancée left him at the altar, he would say something like 'no problem,' or 'happy to help,' or 'anytime.' Instead, because this is the world where Beck Whistler does not function like a normal human being around women after being left at the altar, he says nothing.

Suave.

I motion for her to climb into the truck before I shut the half door to the backseats, then her door.

When I climb into the driver's seat, I'm aware of how close Brooke is. I'm also aware of how she's taking in every little detail of her surroundings as I drive to our houses.

"So," she says through a yawn. "I thought doctors liked the finer things in life—fancy houses, fancy cars, all that."

I grunt.

"I take it you do not. Unless you're hiding something. Like a mega yacht."

"Some things are finer than stuff." I retort. Brooke is silent for a moment, and I take the opportunity to change the subject. "I guess you were tired."

She says nothing, and awkward silence builds.

That was the wrong thing to say.

Finally, she breaks it. "Meemaw." She turns in her seat and addresses June. "Did you hear from Matt? He hasn't called in a while."

Alarm bells ring out *CAUTION* in my brain, but I *am* tired, and I just finished my shift, but didn't June just say she broke up with him?

"I thought you broke up with him," I blurt.

If the silence was awkward before, now it is palpably painful.

"Broke up with Matt?" Brooke asks, enunciating each syllable. "Why on earth would I do that?"

"He seemed like a loser. Didn't even kiss you goodbye."

I chance a quick look at Brooke. Her brow is furrowed, and her eyes blink slowly.

"Why on earth would I break up with and—*ewww, gross—KISS* my *twin* brother? And who told you I broke up with anyone?"

I'm an idiot.

Brooke turns and stares daggers at her grandmother. I keep my eyes on the road, glad that her glare isn't directed at me.

"Meemaw." She draws out the *aw.* "You don't need to discuss my personal life with strangers."

"He's not a stranger, he's a neighbor, and one who wants to get to know you better. I'm just helping."

"Is that what we're calling two a.m. trips to the E.R. now? Helping?" she quips.

"Well, you two certainly aren't doing anything about what's obvious to everyone else."

"I don't need your help, Meemaw. I'm here to help *you*," Brooke huffs and faces forward before turning to stare out her window.

I can't think of anything to say, so I finish the drive home in silence. When I pull into the driveway, I park as close to Miss June's house as I can. I'll have to help her out and carry her up the front porch stairs.

Brooke flings the door open and stomps up the walkway in her fluffy pink slippers, leaving me with June.

"I've never seen her mad before," June murmurs as I exit the car and walk around to her side.

"Somehow, I think you haven't spent a lot of time with her lately," I respond as I lift my arms up to help June down from the truck. I've seen Brooke mad on at least three occasions. The fact that these three occasions have been times when I've directly interacted with her doesn't escape my notice.

June shakes her head, chagrined. "That's true." Her beady blue eyes bore into my own. "I love my granddaughter, and she needs someone with a fire to match her own. So when are you going to take her out?"

"What?" I sputter, dropping my arms to my sides. "I don't know her. I don't date."

"Why not?" June's eyes widen. "You don't *date*? I didn't ask you to *date her*. These days, that just means sleeping together with no commitment at all. I asked you to take her out. And then you *marry* her."

"Woah." My hands fly up into a defensive position. "Miss June. It's not the 1800s. You can't just tell me to marry your granddaughter."

"Pshaw, boy. It's clearer than the sky on a sunny day that you like her goods."

I sigh and scrub a hand along my jawline. Miss June is right. I *do* think Brooke is attractive, but I don't know her well enough to ask her out on a date. And then there's the whole left-at-the-altar mess. I don't touch dating with a ten-foot pole, and I am not about to explain all that to June.

"Miss June, I'll carry you into your house, but you have to promise you'll be good and not cause any more harm to your ankles."

I scoop her into my arms. She's light, and I'm not sure how someone can have such a substantial personality in such a small body.

"If that's the definition of good these days, boy, I think my generation had a lot more fun." She hooks an arm around my neck and pinches my cheek.

9

BROOKE

Dr. Beckett Whistler is pretentious and—there's no other way to put it—insanely attractive. He's also carrying my meddling grandmother up the stairs to her house.

I shake my head as I stand by the front door, holding it open. I must be experiencing temporary insanity because, for a brief moment, I wish that I was in Meemaw's place.

Definitely insane.

He takes Meemaw to the living room couch, where he sets her down gently and elevates her feet with a pillow. He hands her the TV remote and crouches down when she pulls him toward her.

Meemaw whispers something in his ear, and his cheeks turn red.

"No, ma'am," he responds quietly, but loud enough that I hear him.

"Good. Then I approve. You can take Brooke out anytime."

I shake my head vigorously.

"Meemaw!" I interject. "You do not get to choose who I go out with, or when."

"Brookie Cookie, if I'm not allowed to have any fun because of these old bones, you better go have some."

Dr. Whistler stands and stares at me. I know my hair is crazy, and I know I'm wearing pajamas, but today was an extenuating circumstance. It was the *middle of the night.*

"Thank you for your help today, Dr. Whistler. I can assure you we're just fine, and Meemaw is being meddlesome."

His neck cords, and he nods once. I lean against the front door, ready to shut it once he leaves.

With a quick glance at Meemaw, he walks toward me. "Call me if you have any trouble or concerns. I'll be right over." His voice is low, soothing, and I wish he wasn't talking about my grandmother, but I can't let them both know that.

"Thank you, Dr. Whistler. I'll try to keep the patient in line."

He stops just a foot away from the door and meets my eyes with his own chocolate ones. "It's just Beck."

"Ok. Thanks, Dr. Beck."

He grimaces. "No, I mean, just call me Beck, please."

"Ok. Beck."

I gesture for him to walk through the door. I'm ready to take a shower and a nap, but as he steps under the doorway, he stops and turns back to me. His hands clench into fists at his sides, and he doesn't meet my eyes. Instead, he chooses to look at my fuzzy slippers.

"Can-I-take-you-out?" he mumbles.

I gape at him, not computing his words. "Did you just ask me on a date?" Meemaw's chuckle in the background fuels my ire. "Because my meemaw said so? I don't know what game you're playing, but I'm not a charity case."

He turns beet red and shakes his head before dashing out the door, passing his truck, and running up the driveway to his house.

Meemaw calls my name. "Brooke, that man doesn't know what to do with himself and you."

I frown. "Just like everyone else."

"Now that's not true, Brookie. I know a thing or two. He'll come around. And you two will be good together. Just give him a chance."

"Why would I give him a chance, Meemaw? And why on earth would you tell him to ask me out?"

"Because giving good people chances is the right thing to do. I know I raised your momma to teach you that, and I know you know that."

"No, why would *we* be good together? I don't even know him."

"Sometimes, us old folk have hunches, and it's best not to resist them."

I shake my head at Meemaw. "Are you comfortable?"

She nods in response and flips on *Is it Cake?* on the smart TV I upgraded her to the first week I was here.

I set my hands on my hips and look down at her on the couch. "No more baking. Got it? I'm going to shower and take a nap."

Meemaw yawns and settles back against the couch cushions, and though I thought walking away would make the tension dissipate, I'm disappointed that thoughts of Dr. Beckett Whistler follow after me.

10

DR. BECKETT

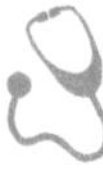

Idiot. *Idiot. Idiot.*

I can't believe I did that. My face burns, my skin itches, my heart beats too fast, and my blood roars in my ears.

I'll blame it on the fact that Brooke and June showed up unexpectedly at the E.R. tonight and that I had to drive them home. It unlocked something I buried years ago, when Addie walked out of my life and left me hanging in the balance.

Women surprising me is not a good thing. I don't like it. I can't really blame Brooke for coming to the E.R. with June either, so my hands are tied. She's *not* after me in the way many women are when they find out I'm a doctor. She's also not *not* interested, if the looks she's given me when she thought I didn't notice mean anything.

And, finding out that she's single, that the man who didn't kiss her in the driveway wasn't her loser boyfriend, but her *twin brother*, I'm … well, yeah. I'm just flummoxed.

I run my fingers through my short hair, wishing for coffee and hours of sleep before I have to head back to the hospital.

I kick off my shoes and flop onto my bed. I don't even bother closing the shades. I'm exhausted, and thinking about Addie fries my nerves in ways that nothing else can.

Hours later, I'm jerked away when my phone buzzes. It's a text from Logan.

Logan

I think you need to come to Billy's.

I grimace. I have no interest in going to the local dive bar and watering hole, even if it *is* our regular routine. I can't drink before work anyway.

Beck

I have to work tonight.

Logan

Not a suggestion. You need to come here.

Beck

I just got up, it was a long night.

Logan

Billy's. Just stop by for a few. Trust me.

Trusting Logan is probably the dumbest thing I'll ever do, but we've been friends since childhood, and he was the one who helped the most after Addie. He called vendors and sweet-talked them into giving me a discount on goods we didn't use. He made the announcement at the church, and he was the one who fielded all the questions from family and friends on both sides of the aisle about what went wrong while I stood there, too shell-shocked to open my mouth.

It's four, which is just enough time to stop by, see Logan and whatever tourist he's picked up this time, grab a bite to eat, and then head to work.

I groan as I stand and stretch out my sore muscles.

A quick bathroom trip and a tiny bit of hair gel later, I've smoothed down the bedhead and look decently presentable.

I throw on black joggers and a dark gray henley under a red plaid flannel. I thrust my badges and ID into my pocket before leaving for Billy's.

Billy's is made of old logs. It's ancient, one of those dive bars that has seen better days and also not seen enough. No one would ever voice an idea to change anything about it, but everyone thinks it would be good to update. All the same, if you were foolhardy enough to voice an idea for improvement, you'd be chased out of town. At the very least, the food's good, even if it's decidedly unhealthy.

I push through the door and enter into the hazy atmosphere. The lighting is so dim that it always takes a moment for my eyes to adjust.

"Beck! Hey, man, over here!" Logan yells, and Ben lifts a cheeseburger in my direction.

I walk across the room, peeling my shoes off the sticky floor with heavy steps. Logan's latest tourist is sitting on his lap and feeding him fries. Ben looks a little disgusted, but it's par for the course with Logan. He collects girlfriends the way some people collect bottle caps.

"Hey," I say as I sit in one of the empty seats at the table. "Why did I need to come down here?"

Just then, a waitress leans over. "What can I get for you? Something to drink?"

I turn to look at her. She's pretty, but my heart doesn't stutter. She's wearing a V-neck, and I keep my eyes trained on her face, even though I know she's trying to show off her cleavage. She's also wearing very short and tight black shorts.

"Water, please," I say and attempt a smile. "And a cheeseburger."

"Ok, but we have three drafts from local breweries on tap tonight—"

I know it's rude, but I cut her off. "Just water. That's all."

She frowns and walks away.

"You have a real touch with the ladies, you know that, right?" Ben elbows me.

I roll my eyes. "Why did you need me down here?"

Logan and Ben meet each other's eyes for a moment before looking away. Ben gives it away when he stares after the waitress.

"Wait." I blink. "You told me to come down here because of *her*?" I hiss the question because I'm not the rudest man in the world and I don't want her to overhear, even though she's nowhere to be seen right now in the crowded bar.

Logan's girlfriend pops up off his lap. "I have to go to the bathroom," she announces before she giggles and pulls Logan in for a lengthy kiss.

Ben makes a retching sound, and I stare at the table, trying to block them out. When she finally scampers off, I look up.

"You two are the worst best friends in the entire world."

"Naw. Don't say that," Ben says as he crams a mouthful of fries.

"Hey." Logan flicks a fry at Ben. "It was *your* idea."

Ben sighs before he presses his palms down on the table. "Listen, man. I just… You never want to meet anyone. And we worry about you. You don't have fun unless we tell you to come with us, and you don't have any of your … personality anymore."

I bristle.

"C'mon, Beck," Logan interjects. "You know it's true. It's been years since Addie, and we want you to come back. We miss the Beck from before."

I stiffen as the waitress puts my burger in front of me.

"Thank you," I growl.

The waitress glares at me before walking away.

"Some things cannot be changed. And some things cannot go back to the way they were before."

"Beck." Ben frowns. "You need to figure something out because … Addie's coming home."

Ben would know. He's Addie's older brother.

I don't say a word, just calmly take a bite of my burger, chew, and swallow. Reach into my pocket and extract my wallet. Fish out a twenty and throw it on the table. Shove my chair out and walk with tingling nerves and all the calmness I can muster back to Billy's door. Inside, my body is combusting.

The aggression has to go somewhere, so I yank the handle toward me and stumble when someone collapses into me.

Instinctively, I reach out to steady them, and my eyes skate over this person's body for signs of injury.

All that is forgotten when I meet the pretty blue eyes of the blonde woman with pink streaks in her hair who's taken up residence in my neighborhood and somehow my heart.

11

BROOKE

Meemaw insisted I drive her ancient Buick to Billy's and grab her a cheeseburger. I could have made one at home, but I was too tired to argue. When I tried to make her promise she wouldn't get into any trouble while I was gone, she practically guffawed.

"Brooke, you need to get into some trouble. I won't get into any *if you promise you will.*"

I don't know what to do with that statement. But that's fine. As long as Meemaw's behaving, I'll be at her beck and call.

Ugh, *Beck.*

Why does that word have such a different meaning now? Why does this have to bring to mind Meemaw's hot doctor neighbor who asked me out because Meemaw told him to? Was that some type of weird mountain man etiquette? Or did he actually want to take me on a date? I didn't really help by insisting I'm not a charity case, but what was I supposed to do? If you're interested in me, just *say* so. And maybe not only because Meemaw told you what to do. And *maybe*, just *maybe*, if you aren't interested in me, say that too.

Would it *kill* our generation to be direct? Sure would clear up a lot of confusion, and probably result in a lot less heartbreak and heartache.

My phone rings with a video call as I put the car in park.

"Hey, Lizzy," I say to my younger sister.

"Hi, Brooke!" She's breathless and flushed. "Guess what?"

"What?"

"I got asked to the homecoming dance by Shane."

Shane's name is squealed at such a high pitch it takes me a moment to figure out who asked her.

"Oh, wow! That's so awesome. So, how did he ask you?"

Lizzy jumps into the whole elaborate dance proposal, and I try not to roll my eyes at the way she makes it sound like this is the start of true love.

"Did you go dress shopping yet?" I ask.

"No, I'm going with Mom on Saturday after the cross-country meet."

"Well, you have to send me pictures of every dress. I want to cast my vote too."

"Ok, but would you *please* tell Matt to make Joey ask Lara?"

"Me tell Matt to tell Joey to ask Lara?"

"Or maybe you just call Joey and tell him to ask Lara?"

"Your best friend, Lara?"

"Yeah, no one's asked her, and I don't want her to be left out."

"Does Joey want to ask Lara?"

"I don't know, but everyone listens to you. Please, Brooke, you'll be my favorite sister forever and ever and ever."

"I'm your only sister."

"Yeah, but are you my favorite?"

I shake my head as I approach Billy's run-down exterior. "I appreciate the attempt at bribery, but I can't force anyone to do anything."

Lizzy sighs. "Just try for me?"

"I'll try, but I have to run."

"Oh, I hope you're meeting a cute guy!"

I snort at my fifteen-year-old sister. "Ha. I'm getting Meemaw a cheeseburger."

I start pushing the door just as she giggles. "With a side of cute guy, right?"

The door flings open with way more force than what I pushed it with, and I stumble forward. My phone drops and skates across the floor, and I find myself caught in the strong and toned arms of…

Dr. Beckett Whistler.

It's hard to see in the dim interior of Billy's, but the light from the door shows his chocolate eyes locked on my face and his mouth set in a deep frown.

His eyes flash with something as he looks me over from head to toe. "Are you hurt?" he asks, his voice low.

I shake my head, unnerved by the way my arms sizzle from the pressure he's placing on my skin.

He swallows, then abruptly lets go. "Good," he grumbles before pushing past me and out the door.

I shake my head, trying to make sense of whatever just happened. Meemaw's neighbor and I are clearly destined to only have odd interactions, and never romantic ones—despite both Matt and Meemaw hinting otherwise.

My vision adjusts to the dim lighting just in time for a large man to approach me, holding my phone out. "Ma'am," he says in a thick mountain accent. "You dropped this."

I smile at him and gratefully accept the phone. "Thanks."

"So…" He draws out the 'o' and tips his head to the door as he stuffs his hands into his front jeans pockets. "Do you know Beck?"

"Not really. He's Meemaw's neighbor."

"Oh," the man breathes. "You're the kid?"

My eyes narrow in suspicion at this man. I take him in. He's dressed in faded blue jeans and a dark green tee shirt with a motorcycle silhouette on the breast pocket. He has curly brown hair that's cut short, and a hint of stubble on his jaw. He's also at least a foot taller than me, and has massive arm muscles. Matt would be jealous.

I raise a brow. "Kid?"

"June MacCord's granddaughter, the kid Beck has been all upset about having to keep an eye on."

I bristle. "I can assure you, Dr. Whistler doesn't have to keep an eye on me at all."

"Somehow I don't think he *isn't* keeping an eye on you." The man sticks out his hand for me to shake. "I'm Ben."

"Brooke Bastion." I grasp his meaty hand in mine.

His hazel eyes narrow. "Brooke," he repeats. "Well, I've known Beck for a long time, and don't mind me saying this, but give him a chance."

I blink. "A chance? I'm just here for a burger for my grandma."

Ben steps back. "So you're a local now."

"I'm here till Meemaw recovers."

"That's local. Come on over, let me introduce you to Logan. He's another friend of Beck and me." He lowers his voice and whispers, "But you have to ignore the tourists he strings along at every opportunity. Beck's not like that at all."

Ben leads the way across the sticky floor to a table in the back corner where another man sits. This one has short but spiky blond hair, wears a white t-shirt with an oar on it, and his arm is wrapped around a woman next to him.

"Hello," the man says, with a tiny bit too much emphasis on the last syllable. The girl gives him a sharp glare. "I'm Logan. This is Trina. How do you know Beck?"

I almost roll my eyes. "Why does everyone assume I know Beck?"

Logan flashes a blindingly white smile. "Apologies. How does Beck know you?"

"She's June's granddaughter," Ben cuts in.

Logan's smile grows to Cheshire cat proportions. "The neighbor."

The woman under Logan's arm stares at me, then tosses her platinum blonde hair over her shoulder and widens her eyes. "You know the grump?"

Ben laughs. "That's one way to put it."

I shrug. "Not really, he's my grandma's neighbor. And I'm here helping Meemaw through her ankle recovery."

"But do you, like, want to know him?" She takes a sip of something fizzy. "He'd be so hot if he wasn't so grumpy. And a doctor. Goodness." Trina fans herself with one hand.

Logan tenses for a moment, then shrugs. "Ahh, but that means us lowly rafting guides with personality get the beautiful women all to ourselves." He hooks her closer with his arm and presses a kiss to her temple. When she turns her face to his, I look away.

Ben's eyes widen, and his attention is studiously not on the two people making out right in front of us.

I'm saved from the awkwardness when a waitress saunters over. "What can I get you?" she asks.

Relieved, I order two burgers to go.

"That will be just a few minutes. Do you want me to bring it to the table or up front to the to-go counter?"

My eyes catch Logan and Trina still lip-locked. "The to-go counter, please," I murmur before giving a general wave and turning on my heel.

I sink into one of the benches by the to-go counter and am surprised when Ben sits next to me. For such a big man, he's light on his feet.

"Sorry about Logan. He doesn't think much these days."

I bite my lip, not sure where this is going. Or why Beck's friends are so interested in me.

"Listen," I say, trying to be direct. "I'm not sure why or how you know I exist. Or what Beck has to do with me. But I'm glad to meet other locals. There's not a lot to do when it's just me and Meemaw, and she's recovering from ankle surgery."

"I get that." Ben nods. "It's just that Beck mentioned you. But he didn't mention *you*. And he's…" He sighs. "I know him well enough to know that he likes you, but he's dense. Anyone with his past would be."

"Past?"

Ben waves a hand. "Forget I mentioned it."

"Ok…"

The waitress arrives with my burgers. "Here you go," she says, passing me the paper bag of food and walking away.

I turn to Ben, who's standing now. "It was nice to meet you. I don't really know what to do with myself, so if you have recommendations for short-term jobs or things to do, that would be great."

"Sure thing. Are you Catholic?"

"No," I say. "I'm a Methodist. Why?"

He bites his lip, clearly hiding something. "No particular reason, just wondering. Also, Miss June knows Logan and me, by the way. Please tell her I'd love some more of her chicken when she's feeling up to it."

This day continues to get stranger, and that's saying something because it started with me in the hospital in my pajamas after Meemaw decided to bake at two in the morning. "Ok. Yeah, sure."

As I turn to leave, I hear Ben mutter, "Beck better not mess this up."

12

BECK

I'm hungry, which is why I'm still in my truck twenty minutes later. I'm contemplating swallowing my pride, returning to Billy's, and ordering another burger. I don't want to see my idiot friends, though. Finally, I give up and am about to head back in, when Brooke comes out. She's carrying a to-go bag.

I shake my head and watch as she crosses the packed-dirt parking lot before climbing into June's old Buick. She puts the car in reverse and starts to creep out of the parking spot when a terrible noise accosts my ears.

Grinding, screeching, scraping.

She slams on the brakes and climbs out of the car, where she crouches down and inspects under the car.

Call it curiosity, chivalry, or the Sunday school lessons about helping someone when they need it come home to roost, or the less altruistic experience of attraction, but I get out of my truck to see what's wrong.

"Brooke?" I ask as I crouch down next to her. She's murmuring something under her breath as one of her hands yanks at her hair.

Her eyes snap to mine.

"What's going on?" I ask.

Tears well in the corner of her eyes. I reach out a hand to touch her shoulder. I startle when she leans into my touch.

She points under the car. "The gas tank fell out."

I look under the car, and there, on the ground, is the gas tank.

"That's not driveable," I say, stating the obvious.

She looks up at me, her blue eyes swimming with tears, and heaves a sob. "I don't know what to do. Usually, I'd call Matt. Or someone. But I can't do that here. I don't really know anyone."

I swear I don't tell my arm to tighten around her shoulder, but it does of its own accord. "You know me." I smile down at her. "I've been told I'm good in a crisis."

The ghost of a smile flits across her face. "Are you making a joke, Dr. Beckett Whistler?"

I shrug. "Did you meet anyone while you were in Billy's?" I ask, knowing full well Ben saw our interaction and immediately had questions that I didn't stick around to answer.

Her eyes narrow, forcing a tear out of the corner. She swipes at it with the back of her hand. "I met your friends."

I grimace. "Yes, well, Logan is a rafting guide, but Ben is a mechanic. He usually sticks to motorcycles, but I can convince him."

"What on earth is a motorcycle mechanic going to do about *that*?" She gestures to the gas tank.

"I have no idea, but Ben will know what to do."

She stands, and I follow. My hand slips off her shoulder, and I'm sad to lose contact with her.

"I guess we better go see what he says."

"Nah. I'll drive you home, and he can come look at it when he's ready."

"Really? But won't he need the key?"

I pull out my phone and fire off a quick text to Ben telling him what happened and that I'm leaving with Brooke.

"You can just leave the key on the windshield."

Brooke arches her eyebrow as one eye widens and the other narrows. The pure skepticism on her face is amusing, if also a bit insulting.

"No one's going to steal it, if that's what you're wondering."

"Oh. I guess not."

"Good," I say as she deposits the key onto the windshield. "I suspect June wants a hot burger, not a cold one."

"I don't think it will be hot when we get back, but it might be warm." Brooke offers a small smile.

She reaches into June's car and extracts the burger bag, then she opens the bag, and the smell of crispy fries hits my nose. She pulls out a handful and holds it out to me, a little smile ticking at the corners of her mouth. "Seems like fair payment for the ride."

Is Brooke Bastion flirting with me?

"Thanks," I say, popping a handful into my mouth and ignoring the way nerve endings misfire as I touch her hand.

"I thought you'd eat healthy as a doctor," she says as we reach the truck.

I open her door for her. "I usually do, but hospitals aren't exactly known for their healthy food. And sometimes a burger at Billy's sounds good."

She starts to buckle in, and my eyes linger on the gentle slope of her neck and shoulder as she twists to click the belt into place. I shake my head to clear whatever is happening here. I need to drive her home, not ogle her. Especially since who knows what June will get up to if left unattended.

I climb into the driver's seat just as I spy Ben and Logan walking out of Billy's together. I do not want to deal with them—not their looks, not their side eyes, not their comments about Brooke and about how I mess everything up because I don't try.

It's not one of my finer moments, but I throw the truck into drive and peel out of the parking lot.

I sense Brooke peering over at me with some confusion. After being calm and gentle and flirting, I'm suddenly driving like a bat out of the netherworld.

Thankfully, she doesn't say anything as I white-knuckle the eight-minute drive home.

I pull into the driveway between June's and my house.

"Thanks, Dr. Beckett," Brooke says as she unbuckles and prepares to hop out.

I put my hand on her arm to stop her. "It's just Beck. Really."

My eyes search hers. She tucks a strand of pink hair behind her ear, and I want to wind it around my finger.

She bites her lower lip.

"Thanks, Beck," she says quietly. Her eyes stay locked on mine, and I don't let go of her arm.

I tug her toward me. She doesn't resist.

Her tongue flicks over her lips, and her eyes narrow as she looks deeply into mine. It's awkward, pulling her closer over the gear shift, but my arms circle her shoulders, and I inhale the scent of her shampoo.

Her hands circle my neck, pressing her palms into the junction of my neck and back.

"Brooke," I whisper, oddly affected by her. "Please go on a date with me. Not because June said so, but because I like you."

She pulls back a little before she leans up and kisses my cheek. "Ok."

I blink, and before I can catch her and pull her in for a proper kiss, she bolts from the truck.

I sit there, confused, as she dashes up the driveway and into June's house.

I asked Brooke on a date, she kissed my cheek, and suddenly a huge elephant lands on my chest.

Addie is coming home. What have I done?

MEEMAW

June MacCord's granddaughter slips through the front door, leaving just the screen door closed and clutching a grease-stained take-out bag.

June leans forward from her perch on the couch. Her ears heard the familiar noise of her neighbor's truck in the driveway, and her keen eyes take in Brooke's face.

"Brookie?" June's voice calls, concern for her granddaughter mounting. "What happened?"

Brooke hesitantly steps forward, unsure how to navigate this conversation with her grandmother. "Your car had trouble."

June's eyebrow arches. "What kind of trouble?"

"Your gas tank fell out."

June laughs. "Who needs that anyway?"

Confusion flashes across Brooke's face. "It's kind of integral to a vehicle."

June sobers. "How did you get home then?"

Brooke flushes, and June knows why, but she waits patiently for Brooke to admit how she arrived back at her mountain home.

"Beck…" Brooke swallows. "Gave me a ride home."

"Is the good doctor just 'Beck' to you now?"

Brooke nods, and June does her best to hide a smile behind her hand.

"Well goodness, me," June supplies. "I guess we better figure out what to do with that car of mine."

Brooke swallows. "I hope you don't mind, Meemaw, but Beck's friend—the mechanic, Ben—is helping."

"You met Benjamin Painter?" June's delight is unconcealed. "He's such a strapping young man. Shame about his sister running off and leaving Beck at the altar all those years ago though. Not sure how they've been friends through all that, but I suppose you also met Logan Manns too? Probably with some tourist woman. That man is all charm. Benjamin is strong and smart, but Beckett…" June trails off, shifting her gaze to the front door, where Doctor Beckett Whistler's shocked face turns away, and he stomps down the porch steps.

13

DR. BECKETT WHISTLER

ddie is coming home, and I asked Brooke on a date. I walk into my house and stare at the crucifix next to the door. I need to push thoughts of Addie aside. And I need to do this. For me.

I like Brooke. I don't want to think I've wasted time wallowing after Addie, but maybe I have. I can't afford to wallow any longer, not when long since dormant romantic feelings have bloomed to new life within me.

Sure, some small part of me wants vengeance, wants to show Addie that I'm doing great without her, but there's a part of me that's bigger and better, that wants to let someone know me without all the damage Addie did in the way.

Maybe one reason I haven't dated since Addie is because it feels like everyone here knows everything about me, except the tourists, and they don't interest me.

Addie wrecked a lot of things. But I won't let her win.

I flip on the bedroom light with more force than necessary, and throw scrubs into my work bag, as well as a set of fresh clothes. I'm lucky that this small regional hospital has facilities for showering, and I like to take advantage of it. Even if it is connected to the gym all the old men in the area frequent.

The zipper on the bag catches and I tug it, letting my frustration pour over me.

I wasn't expecting June to know about Addie and the way she left me at the altar, but I shouldn't be surprised. I'm angry that I didn't think that as soon as she knew my name after I moved in three and a half years ago, she wouldn't call up all the ladies in the church circles and ask questions.

Now I'm angry that Brooke won't get to know me without Addie's influence hanging over my head. Nothing says romance to a woman like, *Hey, I got left at the altar by my fiancée years ago, and I haven't dated since then. Want to go out? Want to settle for me, because she sure didn't.*

June ripped that rug right out from under me. I couldn't see Brooke's face when she learned about *the incident*, but I didn't need to. I saw an entire church's worth of faces who learned about it at the same time as me.

Now, I'm going to see her again. I know that. She's Ben's sister, but I won't give up my friendship with Ben because Addie found me lacking.

Ben's always been tight-lipped about where Addie went and what she was doing, but I know she said she couldn't marry me, and she said it in the loudest, most uncomfortable way possible for everyone involved.

I'm still dealing with the fallout.

I stalk into my kitchen and rummage through the fridge for something to eat. I throw up my hands and growl in frustration as a single brown banana stares back at me.

The storm door banging shut sounds from behind me, and I turn. Brooke stands in the entryway holding the greasy take-out bag from Billy's.

She bites her lip and frowns. "I knocked, but you didn't hear me. I was about to call your name…"

I step toward her slowly.

She eyes me cautiously. "I don't know why you left Meemaw's porch like that, but she insisted I bring you this. Turns out she has a friend bringing us dinner."

"June," I grumble as I take the bag from Brooke's outstretched hand.

Brooke stares at me, her eyes wide and questioning, the gray tile of my entryway reflected in them.

"Look, Brooke," I start, then stop. I rub my fingers over my beard, unsure where to go from here. "June was matchmaking today. She must have seen me leave, and she knows I usually go to Billy's with Ben and Logan before my shift on Thursday."

"Oh," she breathes. "Ok. I'll tell her to stop meddling." She turns to leave, and I have to stop her. I put my hand out to stop her, holding the door knob so she can't leave yet.

"I'm…" I blink at the tears in Brooke's eyes. "Why are you crying, Brooke?"

"I thought maybe you really did want to go on a date with me." She looks down at the floor. "It's ok, though, you don't have to do anything you don't want to do."

I scratch my head. She thinks I don't want to date her? I messed this up. "It's not that. June … mentioned something that I was hoping to not have you know."

Brooke's eyes widen, and I know I have to tell her. If I'm interested in dating again—and I am—then I need to say it. I need to tell the story in a way that won't come back to bite me.

"Addie is Ben's sister. We were engaged. She didn't show up at our wedding. And everyone here knows that. I was hoping to maybe ease into dating without that over my head. It's not really something I enjoy talking about, and it's not a great way to start off a relationship."

"Is that the worst thing in your past?" Brooke asks.

I think for a moment. "Yeah, it pretty much is."

She steps closer to me, till there's just an inch of space between us. My hand tenses on the doorknob.

"I don't know anything about Addie, or why she did that, but it seems like her loss."

I swallow, wanting to pull Brooke in and kiss her but knowing that it's not time to do that, not now. "Thank you."

Her eyes narrow at the lame response. I'm not sure what to say to anyone about Addie, least of all myself, but Brooke's kindness makes me even more awkward.

"So you do want to go on a date with me?" she asks.

I nod, tongue-tied.

"When?"

Her question unlocks my frozen tongue and brain, and I suddenly have an idea.

"Tomorrow? Want to hike at ten?"

"I'd love to," she says as she places her hand over mine on the doorknob. Her palm is cool and soft, and I'm tempted to catch it with my other hand just to hold it longer, but she twists her hand on top of mine, and the door springs open.

She walks into the cooling evening air before I can understand what just happened.

I breathe out a prayer. "Lord, I don't know what you're doing, but I like her. Please don't let me mess this up."

14

BROOKE

What does one wear on a hiking date with their attractive neighbor? Technically, their meemaw's neighbor, but semantics.

I settle on a pair of black athletic capris, a pink short sleeve top, and a light pink jacket. It's still cool in the mornings here in the mountains. When I told Meemaw about our date last evening, she laughed and clapped her hands together like a child.

"I knew it!" she exclaimed and then turned to her friend who brought us dinner—Miss Essie—and told her all about how I would be getting married before long.

It was a lot. But part of me really wants to believe that it will be that way. That Beck and I might work out. I was the little girl who dreamed of being a princess, rescued by her prince on a white horse. Beck isn't the prince I imagined, but I'm willing to shove my childish imaginings aside and experience real life, and a real date, with Beck.

A knock on the front door startles Meemaw awake from where she's been dozing on the couch.

I spring up off the floral cushion and smooth out the non-existent wrinkles from my athletic outfit. When I open the door, Beck stands there with his hat in one hand and a bouquet of flowers in the other. I can't see his full face over the bouquet, but his eyes are bright, and if I had to guess, he's smiling.

"Miss June," he says to Meemaw as I usher him inside. "These are for you." He shows her the flowers, and she smiles.

"He's a gentleman, Brooke." She nods in approval at me.

"I try," Beck says before turning back to me. As I see his face, I realize he shaved.

He extends the flowers to me, and I take them and put them in a vase for Meemaw. When I return, Beck is sitting on the couch next to Meemaw, asking her questions about her ankle and her recovery.

"How are you getting around now? Any pain?"

"No, no pain, just using that silly scooter thing you brought over."

Beck brought the scooter over?

He nods solemnly. "And you're not using the scooter as a step stool, right?"

Meemaw frowns. "This bossy doctor I know told me not to."

I laugh at their banter. I had thought that Beck was annoyed by Meemaw, but it seems that under that gruffness, there's a heart of gold.

"You'll be alright while I'm gone?" I ask Meemaw while I set the vase of flowers and a glass of water by her.

"Yes, stop worrying about me."

"But you'll call if you need anything, right?"

"Brookie, I am *not* about to ruin your date. I need my granddaughter to get married because so far, none of my grandchildren have. I'm getting up there in years and only have so many left where I can do all those new-fangled dances like the Macarena."

Visions of Meemaw doing the Macarena fly through my mind, and it's all I can do to not snort in laughter. A glance at Beck shows his hand curled into a fist and covering his mouth. He's also struggling not to laugh.

"I'm glad you're doing better, Miss June," Beck says as he stands up from the couch. "I'll have her back by two this afternoon."

"As long as there's a marriage at the end of this, any time you bring her home is fine."

Beck's cheeks flush, and I intervene. "I'll be back by two, Meemaw, and call if you need anything."

Beck clears his throat. "You can call Ben if you need something right away. He's not working this morning ... if for some reason we don't have service on the trail."

"Go on now, you two, enough hen pecking at me."

I shrug as Beck looks at me, his eyes snagging on my long braid with the pink streaks before he looks down at my feet. I'm not wearing any shoes because I'm inside.

"You need some good shoes," Beck says as we walk to the door with an awkward amount of space between us.

"I have some hiking boots on the porch."

"Good."

I open the door and step onto the porch as Meemaw calls out, "You two need to figure out how to talk to each other. It's like dry cornbread without butter *or* honey listening to you."

My entire face flushes at Meemaw's comment as I shut the door on my meddlesome grandmother's commentary. I shove my feet into the hiking boots I left by the door and grab the bag I left next to them. It's an over-the-shoulder single-strap backpack with my ID, phone, debit card, and a snack, and of course it's pink.

"You never said where we're going." I look up from my crouched position as I tie the bright pink laces of my hiking boots.

Beck's brow furrows. "Is everything you own pink?"

I blink at him. That was not the response I expected. "No, not everything, but it is my favorite color, so if I have a choice, I choose pink."

He nods once. "I thought I'd take you to Long Point. It's touristy, but it's the best view of the bridge."

"Oh, do we get to drive across the bridge to get there?"

"Yeah," Beck responds before rubbing his hand on his bare chin. It's like he can't believe the beard is gone either. "You won't see much from the bridge while we're driving, but if you're here for Bridge Day…"

"Bridge Day?"

"It's an annual day every year in October. The Bridge closes to traffic, and people BASE jump and do all sorts of really dangerous stunts that I can't condone as an E.R. doctor, but it's also a big festival and loads of fun. I haven't been in years, but if you're still here, I could show you around."

I'm not sure I've ever heard him say so many words at one time, and the undercurrent of nervousness in his voice makes butterflies take flight in my stomach.

"Sounds fun." I smile at him and am rewarded when his smile lights his eyes. It's a different look, seeing him without the beard, but I really like it.

We reach his truck, and he opens the door for me. I inhale his woodsy, soapy scent, and also catch a whiff of something I can't identify. It's familiar, but foreign.

I buckle in as Beck crosses in front of the truck and taps the hood while he passes by.

I watch the muscles in his forearms flex as he clicks the buckle into place, starts the truck, and pulls away from the drive.

15

DR. BECK

My face feels naked. I probably shouldn't have shaved this morning, but I stood in my outdated pink bathroom, stared at my reflection, and decided that if I was really going to try dating again, I needed to make some changes. The easiest one I could think of at the moment was losing the beard. I've hidden behind it for years. I grew it after Addie left, and it's been something that shielded me from everything and everyone. But, as I discovered through my morning prayer, if I'm going to do this, if I'm going to put myself out there and feel *feelings* for someone, I might as well do it all the way.

Sure, shaving was metaphorical, but it was also different, and it felt right.

Brooke is quiet, but there's a nervousness in her posture. Her hands are tucked under her arms in a way that makes me think she might be cold. For the first time *ever*, I wish I had a newer truck, the kind with heated seats that I could offer to turn on for her.

"You cold?" I ask, and my voice is scratchy.

Brooke angles her face to look at me. "A little. I'll be ok when we get moving though."

I'm silent for a minute.

"Wasn't this area a big part of the Civil War?" she asks.

Oh, thank goodness. A topic I can actually talk about.

I breathe out a sigh of relief.

"Yes," I say, then point to a historical marker along the side of the road. "There's tons of history here. It's a big part of the area. Is that something you … like?"

She directs her gaze out her window at the passing landscape, but she responds loud enough that I hear her over the roar of the truck. "Yes. It's my favorite genre to read—historical fiction. We studied the Civil War in seventh grade and again in high school. Never did a lot of World War II in school, though, so I've learned a lot about that on my own since college."

"Maybe you'd have some book recommendations for me, then." On the outside, I'm cool, collected, and calm, but on the inside, *who is this and where has Beck gone?* I do like to read, but I rarely have time, and I've never picked up a World War II book—ever.

"You like to read?" Brooke asks, and there's a little bit of surprise in her voice.

"Yeah. I don't get a lot of time to do it, but I enjoy it when I can."

She nods, and I catch the movement from my periphery.

"Here's the bridge," I say as I turn onto the main road and join the traffic zipping across the New River below. I stay in the outside lane so she can see some of the scenery as we cross, but it takes only about thirty seconds, so she won't see much.

"Wow," she breathes. "I wish I could see more for longer. It must have been amazing to be building this."

"Definitely," I say, and then inspiration strikes me. I tuck it away in the back of my mind, but I already know what to do for another date, if she'll allow me to take her on one.

Don't get ahead of yourself, Beck. She might not choose you.

We're silent for a while as I drive through the hairpin turns, but it's not uncomfortable. Brooke is simply looking at everything, and I want to know what she thinks. I try to see this area as a newcomer, as she does. Houses cling to the sides of the mountains, some with well-kept yards, others without. Poverty is apparent, but so is wealth. There's not much rhyme or reason to it, but it's how it is in Appalachia.

"Michigan must be different from here," I comment, breaking the silence.

"Definitely," Brooke responds, but doesn't offer anything else. I want to know about where she grew up. I want to know how she sees the world, how she sees this place, my home, but voicing those questions feels too heavy and too risky.

I turn the truck into the trailhead parking lot.

"We're here," I announce with a smile, even though my heart is hammering faster than a jackhammer. I haven't been on a date in so long, I don't know what to do. I don't know what Brooke expects. I'm second-guessing anything and everything.

I unbuckle and hop out of the truck, grabbing a backpack from the bed on my way to Brooke's door. I shouldn't be surprised when she's already out of the truck by the time I get to her door.

I frown as she pulls her pink backpack over her shoulders. It's very small and very feminine.

"Do you have everything you need?" I ask.

"I think so. This isn't an all-day hike, right?"

I shake my head. I walk to the trailhead, but before I do, I slip a ginger candy in my mouth.

Brooke pulls out her phone and snaps a picture of the sign before slipping it back into her pocket.

"I like to take pictures of things to put into a scrapbook." She shrugs as I raise my eyebrows. The sign is completely ordinary, but something about her wanting to remember this moment makes my heart thrum.

We walk a few steps stiffly side by side before she reaches over and grabs my right hand with her left one.

Her hand is cool and comforting and soft. There are a few calluses there too. More than anything, I'm grateful for her lead.

"You nervous, Dr. Beck?" she teases as she looks at my eyes with amusement.

"You have no idea," I say back to her, swallowing. "I'm a little bit…" I pause while I think about the right word. "Out of practice on dates."

"I think you're doing great," she says generously. I know I'm *not* doing great at this, but I really like Brooke. I don't want to mess this up.

"Oh!" she exclaims. "Look, a snake!"

I follow where she points with her right hand and see a black snake sunning on a rock to the side of the trail. My mouth drops open. This is a red flag for me.

"Do you like snakes?" I ask, alarmed.

"Not at all," she says back with a laugh. "But that one's over there. And we rarely see them in Michigan."

Michigan suddenly sounds a lot better than the frigid, barren polar wasteland I've been envisioning.

"Do you like snakes?" she asks.

"Not even a little bit. Too many horror stories to count in the E.R., and also my sister…"

"You have a sister?"

"Yes." I think about what to say next, because it's clear Brooke expects more than just a one-word answer here. I inhale, trying to find courage. "Her name is Beatrice, but she goes by Bea. She's three years older than me, so she's thirty-one, and a herpetologist. She always loved snakes, and she forced me to learn far too much about them when we were kids. She's studying them in the Amazon or something right now."

Brooke's brow furrows and she blinks deliberately. Twice. "Your sister is studying snakes? In the Amazon?"

I nod, unsure of what else to say about Bea and her love of reptiles as Brooke blinks.

"Okay." She draws out the last syllable and sighs. I wish I was better at conversation, but it's a skill I've not honed. Solving medical emergencies? Yes. Talking to people? No.

"So, what made you want to be a doctor?" she asks.

She's having mercy on me. At least, I hope it's mercy and not pity. *I can do this.*

"I always wanted to help people. My dad … he died when I was ten, and he was always telling me to help whoever I could." I wait for the crack in my heart that always comes along with mentioning Dad to come, but it doesn't. "I was never great with words and talking to people, but I still wanted to help them."

"I get that sense," Brooke responds, and there's a teasing chiding in her voice that makes me think I should probably say more. She sobers. "I'm sorry for your loss."

I open my mouth once, close it, open it again, and stop on the trail to face her, the sincerity in her voice giving rise to my own emotions bubbling up. "I haven't really had a lot to say to anyone in a long time."

Brooke's eyes soften, and she places a hand on my forearm. "I've always had a lot to say, but I like to listen too."

Her eyes are pleading with me for something, and I don't know what she wants, but I desperately want to give it to her.

Addie's voice comes unbidden into my mind. *You never talk, Beck. You never carry a conversation.*

Could that be what Brooke wants? I put my foot in my mouth when I assumed her twin was her boyfriend. I probably should clear that elephant out of the National Park.

"So, you have a twin?" I start down the path and she keeps stride next to me, so I lean over and take her hand in mine. It's warm and solid and comforting.

She inhales a shaky breath, and I'm a little relieved that I affect her too.

"Yeah. Matt. He's my best friend. But that's led to some awkwardness over the years, like when my grandma's neighbor assumed we were boyfriend and girlfriend instead of brother and sister."

"Hey, in my defense, it was an easy mistake to make."

She huffs. "I hope not!"

"I was jealous."

Her eyes turn to look at me, and there's a hint of amusement playing behind in the sparkle. "Jealous. Of my twin brother."

"I just knew that I'd treat you better if you were my girlfriend. I definitely would have kissed you goodbye."

Brooke stops and blinks deliberately. "Is that what this is?"

In for a penny, out for a pound.

"It's what I'd like it to be."

Her lips form a wry smile, and then she nods. "We'll see. But I like the sound of that."

My steps feel just a little lighter as we walk hand in hand down the trail.

16

BROOKE

eck is a little like a clam. Or is it an oyster? He's quiet, and not the easiest person to talk to, unless you're Meemaw and being ridiculous, but when you get him to open up, pearls of humor and sincerity are right there. He told me he lost his dad, but I sense he doesn't want to linger on that, so I don't probe.

Beck walks with sure steps down the well-worn trail. We reach a rhododendron hell, which is a strange name, but really what the early settlers to the area called the patches of mountain thick with woody, viny, massive plants. A sign explains the name, and I, in true nature, stop to read it. I want to soak up every piece of information about this place.

Beck doesn't complain. He doesn't tug my hand or usher me away from the sign as I take my time reading it. And honestly, I'm testing him a little, because I've been done reading this sign for a minute, and I'm still pretending to read it. He stands next to me, my hand in his, and for someone who is used to rushing around because every second matters in his line of work, he's acting like he has all the time in the world—like I could stand here and stare at this sign for the next twenty hours, and it would be fine with him.

I make eye contact with Beck. He smiles down at me, a crooked, bemused smile on his face and a knowing glint in his eye. "Rhododendron hells are that interesting?" he teases in that low voice, and I know I've been caught.

"Fascinating," I respond. "I'm just glad to know you're not the impatient—"

My thoughts are interrupted by shouts farther down the trail.

"Help! We need help! Call an ambulance!"

Beck looks at me for a moment, blinks rapidly, then drops my hand and runs toward the voices.

I stare at my hand for a moment, too stunned to move, as I process. It only takes a second before I understand why he ran. I take off after Beck.

Beck is faster than me, and he knows where he's going. I don't. By the time I find him at the end of the trail, on an outcrop of rocks, he's kneeling on the ground and performing CPR on an older woman. Three other women stand around her, their pale faces framed by gray hair.

I stand back, transfixed by Beck. He doesn't waver. He doesn't stop. He continues for what feels like hours until finally we hear the sound of an ambulance, and EMTs come running down the path with a stretcher. They pull an emergency defibrillator out and take over.

Beck watches as they perform their job, eventually lifting the woman onto the stretcher and murmuring to the group of women. One of the EMTs approaches Beck.

"Dr. Whistler?" the man with a chocolate brown beard down to his stomach asks.

Beck nods, but his face is pale. He's drenched in sweat.

"You saved her life."

Beck nods again, not saying anything in response.

The EMT leads the three women back up the trail as they follow their friend.

Beck sits on the ground, taking shaky breaths as he leans his head against his knees and closes his eyes. I sit next to him, not sure what to do or what to say to him. He's a legitimate hero—he just saved a woman's life. But I sense he doesn't want me to say that to him right now.

Words might have always come easily to me, but this is a situation where words aren't right. We've only ever held hands. This is our first date. And yet…

I don't let myself second-guess it. I scoot closer to Beck, close enough that our hips touch. Then, I slide my arm around him.

He startles at the touch, but picks his head up and locks his eyes on mine before leaning his head on my shoulder.

As his breaths even out, I'm able to appreciate the view for the first time. I let out a low whistle. The outcrop we're sitting on is a ledge at the edge of a mountain that provides us with a view of the New River below and the New River Gorge Bridge above. The trees are vibrant green, the majesty and height of the mountains on either side of the gorge on full display.

Beck picks his head up off my shoulder at the sound I made. "Do you like it?" he asks, like I'd be more impressed with the view than by his life-saving actions.

"I like everything I've seen today," I answer with honesty.

He gives a small smile and then stands, extending a hand to me. I grasp it without hesitation. When I stand next to him, he looks at me, then quickly looks away. "I…" He scrubs a hand down his face. "I … uh. I didn't mean to leave you back there."

Blinking away surprise at his nervousness, I squeeze his hand tighter with my own and offer the highest praise I can think of. "I thought you were heroic."

Beck flinches.

17

DR. BECK

Heroic. It's a nice word. But not when it's been sneered at you. Repeatedly.

I can't help but bristle at words that hurt. Beside me, Brooke drops my hand, stands, and walks farther out on the ledge. She keeps going closer to the edge, and my heart dives.

"Brooke," I whisper-call, trying not to alarm her. She is on the precipice, and you cannot survive a fall from this height.

Brooke looks over her shoulder with a crinkled brow and a frown, then plops down.

I approach slowly and ease down next to her.

I swallow. "Hero wasn't a nice word in … uh … Addie's vocabulary."

Brooke brings her knees to her chest and wraps her arm around her shins. She rests her cheek on her kneecap and fixes me with a wide-eyed gaze. A wisp of pink-streaked hair escapes her braid, and I impulsively tuck it behind her ear. She startles a bit at the contact, but then chews her lip. I take it as a good sign that she doesn't smack my hand away.

When she speaks, her response isn't what I expected. "I don't really like heights."

"Ok," I say. But then, because I'm not skilled at talking to pretty women unless they're having a medical emergency, I state the obvious. "But you're sitting at the very edge of a rock ledge that's hundreds of feet in the air."

"That's the point." She picks her head up and stretches her neck from side to side. "I do things that scare me. And I find I can enjoy them with enough practice."

I don't fully understand the lesson, but I know there's one here. It's like Aesop and his fables. If only I had ever understood what the fables taught. It's like Brooke is giving me pieces to a puzzle, but the only picture I have is the one I imagined the puzzle would look like, and the pieces aren't fitting together.

I do the only thing I can in this situation—give her a single nod to show I heard her.

She smiles softly, then shivers and scoots back from the edge until she's firmly in the center of the rock formation. "That was enough exposure therapy for me today."

I can't help it. I'm a serious man, but there is something so charming about Brooke, with her pink hair and her wide eyes and her gorgeous smile that ... I laugh. Not a chuckle, but a real laugh. The kind of laugh that I haven't let out in four years, three months, elev—

But why bother counting?

Brooke arches an eyebrow and smirks. "Find something funny about my completely rational fear?" she teases.

"Yeah," I say, walking toward her. "It's that I was just thinking that I haven't wanted to meet anyone for a long time, and then it's my ridiculous neighbor's granddaughter who swoops in, all gorgeous, and is the first person to make me laugh in over four years."

"Four years without laughing?" She frowns. "I wasn't trying to be funny."

"That's the thing, though, Brooke," I say, ambling closer and wrapping her hand in mine. "You didn't have to try."

She's quiet for a moment, her eyes turning to the vista before us. I'm sweaty and sticky, and spent half our date performing CPR on a random stranger, but she didn't think that was a problem. She made me laugh with her joke about exposure therapy. She's completely herself.

I allow myself to think that maybe she *really* thought I was heroic. My chest inflates with hope.

She didn't mind the sweat before when she hugged me after everything, and I have the urge to pull her into my arms, but she drops my hand, pulls her phone out, and begins taking pictures of the view.

The moment passes like the beat of a butterfly's wings.

It's an incredible panorama, I'll give her that, but it's not the best thing I've seen today.

"Here." I hold out my hand for her phone.

"Hmm?" she says, not turning around.

"Let me take one with you in it."

"A little bold there, Dr. Whistler," she teases over her shoulder.

I arch a brow and shake my head at her teasing, holding my hand again out for her phone.

Brooke passes it to me, but as she does, a new voice meets my ears.

"I can take it for y'all."

"That would be great." Brooke beams a huge smile at the woman who said it.

I turn slowly toward the voice. I know my ears heard it, but maybe my brain is warping sound or something. It has to be a glitch in the matrix. It has to be.

Brooke's arm snakes around my waist as she poses for the picture, but I can't move. I can't say a single word.

"Beck?" Brooke and Addie say at the same time.

18

BROOKE

I was too forward. I shouldn't have put my arm around Beck's waist for the picture. He wasn't ready for that. It's clear as day on his face when I touch him and he stiffens like a starched collar.

I drop my arm and try to break the tension.

"Oh, you know each other?" I ask, because I am an idiot who cannot put two and two together.

Beck's face is granite. I only know him at a surface level right now, but I know him enough to see that the light in his eyes is gone. It's like he's running, or hiding, or maybe both.

"Yeah, you could say that." The petite woman with impossibly straight and shiny long black hair and perfectly manicured nails scoffs. Her brown eyes narrow as she looks Beck up and down in a predatory way. I don't like it one bit.

"Beck?" I whisper.

His eyes snap to mine, and he sighs. "Addie," he says, looking at me but addressing the woman. "This is my friend, Brooke. Brooke, this is Addie."

I bristle at the word friend, then blink. This is Addie? The woman Beck wanted to marry. The woman who planned a wedding with him and left him at the altar.

I mentally do a calculation of how I physically compare to her, and I come up short.

Though everything in me wants to be rude, I stick out my hand. "Nice to meet you."

Sometimes I hate having manners. It would be so much easier if I didn't know I needed to treat everyone with kindness and respect. For better or for worse, the Golden Rule has stuck with me from years of Sunday school and sermons.

Addie shakes my hand briefly. "So, you two are friends?" she questions.

That's weird. Why isn't she asking Beck?

She laughs, a tinkly, airy sound with no mirth, as I look to Beck for an answer. "Oh, don't bother trying to get Beck to talk. He doesn't do that. It's up to you to give me the scoop on"—she surveys the awkward space between Beck and me, and smirks while she waves her perfectly manicured fingers—"whatever this is."

Beck's Adam's apple bobs.

My heart beats in double time. This man is strong and confident, and just saved a woman's life earlier today. Yet, here he is, on a rock ledge, and this woman has reduced him to rubble.

Anger bubbles up from my stomach.

How can one woman do this to a man? How can a woman beat a good man down like this?

"Actually, Addie." I make sure to say her name, giving her a clue that I know a bit about her. "We're on a date. And we'd love that picture now."

In what might be the most unhinged moment of my life, I stand on my tiptoes, put my arms around Beck's neck, and lean in to kiss his cheek. While I'm by Beck's ear, I whisper, "Don't let her get to you."

He startles and turns to face me, brushing our noses together.

"Thanks," he whispers in return.

I smile, then quickly sink back down to my heels, slip my hand into Beck's, and hold my other hand out for my phone as I stare Addie down.

Addie's narrowed eyes and tight-lipped frown would have clued me in to the kind of person she is, but even more so, the words she speaks reveal the true colors of her heart.

"Good luck with that, honey." She sneers as she places the phone in my hand.

The that being Beck, apparently. I resist the urge to roll my eyes.

I pocket my phone and tug Beck's hand, leading him back to the trail. I've always been a take-charge type of person, and I was hoping I wouldn't have to be with Beck, but he remains silent for the walk back to his car, and I can't think of anything to say.

Parked next to Beck's old truck is a shiny black SUV with a luxury brand decal on the back. I bite my lip to stop myself from saying anything because that car—it has to be Addie's.

Beck ignores the vehicle next to his truck and silently opens my door before crossing in front of the truck and climbing into his own seat.

He sits, silent for a breath, as he stares straight ahead at the edge of the parking lot, then puts his arm around the back of the passenger seat, turns his head, and backs out of the parking space.

Thoughts fly through my head at a mile a minute, but the only one I would actually say is the one that sticks in my throat. Whatever just happened at Long Point, no matter how uncomfortable that situation made me, Beck is hurting, and I can't bring myself to say, So that's the woman who left you at the altar? *Good riddance.*

The tension in the truck is too much, and without realizing it, I begin to pull on my hair.

Beck's eyes are firmly planted on the road when he breaks the suffocating silence. "You shouldn't do that."

"What?" I try to meet his gaze, but it's stubbornly fixed ahead.

"Your hair."

I pull my hand away, staring at it as if it has a mind of its own.

"Oh," I breathe. "I just—I do it when I'm nervous. I don't even realize I'm doing it some—"

I break off in mid-sentence as Beck makes a sudden turn into a small church parking lot. He shifts the truck into park before scrubbing a hand over his face. The calloused skin of his palm makes a rasping noise against the softness of his freshly shaven face. He looks at me, brown eyes meeting mine with a plea for understanding in them.

I give him a small smile and nod, watching as he fights for words.

"I…" He sighs. "That's Addie."

I sit in quiet expectation. He has something more to say—I can see it in the set of his jaw, the way he's holding his shoulders.

"She … uh … she and I…" He turns to look out the driver's side window so I can't see his face anymore. His pain is palpable, and I want him to know he can share it. It's instinctive, putting my hand on his arm, but he must not have expected it because he turns back to me, and I'm surprised by the tears in his eyes.

"Addie changed. I knew her as a kid. She's Ben's younger sister, and we … always liked each other. I don't know what happened, but there were … signs that we weren't really a good match. And I forced it because everyone expected us to get engaged and married and have seven kids."

I blink back in surprise. "You're blaming her leaving you at the altar on you?" I ask before I've comprehended how insensitive that question is for a first date.

Beck's brow furrows into deep creases. "No. Yes. Maybe?" He sighs. "I just wanted you to know that I was part of the problem."

I squeeze his arm. "I don't know anything except what I've been told about it, and based on what I saw just now, I don't think you were the problem, Beck."

He looks into my eyes with such mournfulness that I'm tempted to climb over and kiss him until he cheers up, but I am not going to do that.

Instead, he opens his mouth, closes it, and begins driving the truck out of the church parking lot. Beck doesn't say a single word for the rest of the drive.

The clock on the dashboard says one p.m., and I'm disappointed when he turns into Meemaw's driveway, but I also understand. From what I've gathered, Beck hasn't seen Addie in years. It was a lot for me to process, let alone for him.

Beck extracts the keys from the ignition before he blinks two long, slow blinks. "Brooke. I'm sorry."

I shrug. "It's ok. You couldn't have controlled when and where she showed up."

Beck curls his lower lip under his top teeth. "No, Brooke. I'm … this isn't going to work."

"What?"

"I can't date you."

Alarm bells ring.

This is a breakup speech. And after one date. I've reached a new low.

The anger that bubbled up earlier at Addie didn't dissipate; it's still there boiling under the surface.

"Don't you dare give up." I hurl the words at his face, and he shrinks back away from the voracity in my voice. "You don't have to date me, but you certainly don't have to let her hang over you this way anymore."

I slide my phone out and flip to the picture Addie took of us, pushing the screen close to his eyes.

Surprise registers on his face as he takes in the image of us on Long Point. My arms around his neck, hands clasped loosely together, and his own hand resting on my upper arm as our noses brush together, framed by the breathtaking scenery behind us. It's an image worthy of a postcard or a save-the-date wedding magnet. In the heyday of Facebook profile pictures, this one would have been a winner.

"Don't give up," I admonish again, and then I hop out of the truck before he can say another word.

19

BECK

"D on't you dare give up." Brooke's blue eyes fix my own with such fire that I shrink away from her. Before I can regain my bearings, Brooke pushes the picture Addie took of us in front of me.

That picture is, in a word, stunning. But I'm digesting everything in slow motion, and it's impossible to make sense of what she's saying or doing.

How could Addie have taken that picture? How could Addie have been right there? Ben said she was coming home soon, but he didn't say when.

Brooke is out of the truck before I can register my internal thoughts with my external actions, let alone before I can respond to her.

I sit for a moment, stunned, as I watch her walk away. Brooke's parting words reverberate through my ears.

Don't give up.

My brain is not in sync with my body today, because before I can overthink it, I'm out of the truck and jogging up the pathway and yelling, "Brooke, wait!"

She stops at the top of June's porch and turns slowly, her pink-streaked braid flipping over her shoulder. Her gaze connects with mine as I stand on the bottom step of the porch.

"I'm sorry. I wasn't expecting to see her today, or anytime, really, and I don't want to give up."

Brooke smiles softly. "You don't have to give up."

"Yeah, but you shouldn't have had to deal with that on our first date."

Brooke's eyes widen. "Our first date, as in one of many, or as in the only one?"

"Could I take you on another one? One where I guarantee there won't be … uh … *her* … there?"

"What happened to '*I can't date you*'?" Brooke probes. Her eyes don't shy away from mine. This is a woman who wants total honesty. And this is a woman I *want* to be totally honest with.

"I was giving up. And you called me out on it."

"But what were you giving up on?"

I swallow. My throat must have a thousand jagged pieces of glass lodged in it.

She wants total honesty. She deserves total honesty.

"I was giving up on ever being happy. It didn't have anything to do with you."

"But didn't it?" she challenges. "I mean, you took me on one date and then told me you couldn't date me, and now you want to date me again?"

"Brooke." I step closer to her. "I'm not the smartest person when it comes to women." Her eyes twinkle at the self-deprecation lacing my voice, so I take the next step, bringing me to eye level with her. "Please, may I take you on another date that doesn't have all that awkwardness?"

A shadow of something flashes over Brooke's face, but it passes in a moment. "Ok. But you have to promise me that you'll remember something."

"Anything."

"I am not, have never been, and never will be Addie."

I can't help it. I grin as I take in Brooke's pink hair, her worn hiking boots, clothes that fit but aren't luxury brands and have clearly been worn before, and the way she challenged me to be a better man despite only going on one date. Brooke and Addie are as different from each other as night and day.

"I think I can remember that."

Brooke opens her mouth, then snaps it shut as her stomach rumbles what sounds like a dinosaur wail. Finally, she opens it again. "Are you hungry? We didn't ever eat a snack, and it's past my lunch time."

"Clearly," I tease before answering her seriously, "I'm starving."

She inhales, then blows out a breath. "Then, come on in. Meemaw will probably have a million inappropriate questions for us, but she'll be so thrilled to have you."

I make up my mind right then and there to answer every single one of June MacCord's inappropriate questions honestly because Brooke is absolutely right. June is going to ask questions, and there will be no filter.

Brooke unlaces her hiking boots and leaves them on the porch, so I do the same, then open the door and cross the threshold into June's house. Brooke disappears into the kitchen. June sits on the couch, a knowing eyebrow cocked.

"Didn't think I'd be here, did you, young man?" She lets the implication of Brooke and I being unsupervised hang between us while she smirks.

"Of course I knew you'd be here, Miss June," I retort. "I had to come see how my favorite neighbor is doing."

"Mmmhmmm." She shakes her head. "I'm on to you. That's my granddaughter. And if I catch wind of any hanky-panky, you'll be marrying her."

"Got your shotgun all ready?" I quip.

"Absolutely," she says loudly before she lowers her voice. "I need a granddaughter to get married, so please hanky-panky. I always wanted to chase a man with ol' Eddie."

"Old Eddie?"

"My grandpappy's shotgun." She bobs her head. "Has a sawed-off barrel and everything."

"That's illegal."

"Eh. What the government don't know won't hurt 'em."

I cross the room to sit by June on the couch. "Listen, Miss June," I say quietly. "I have no idea where things are going to go with me and Brooke, but I like her a lot. And I haven't felt that way about anyone since…" I release a breath. "I promise that I think of Brooke as marriage material, and I won't do anything to disrespect her."

"Good." She gives a curt nod. "Now go help her make lunch. A woman needs to see a man capable of domestic tasks if you're going to have any chance of that hanky-panky."

This woman is eccentric, but I understand her. She loves Brooke fiercely, and wants her to be happy. Why she thinks Brooke would be happy with me is a mystery, but I'll give June the benefit of her elder years.

I push up from the couch and begin walking to the kitchen, where I can hear Brooke humming. I stop midway and turn to June. "You don't really have a sawed-off barrel shotgun, do you?"

All June does is wink.

MEEMAW

June MacCord has several life ambitions, but one of them is to attend the wedding of at least one of her grandchildren. Admitting her age is something she does, if only begrudgingly. With her recent injuries, June begins to suspect she isn't as spry as she once was.

Ol' Eddie does indeed exist, although this version does not have a sawed-off barrel, and June knows she'd never use it on Beckett. Still, the tease was fun, and she has no regrets about bringing up marriage between her handsome doctor neighbor and her granddaughter on their first date.

Her hearing isn't what it once was, but it's still surprisingly good for someone who's in their seventies. She listens to the sounds coming from the kitchen, where her granddaughter prepares lunch. She sinks her head back into the couch pillows and closes her eyes, straining to hear the doctor's low rumble and her granddaughter's quiet murmur.

June's lips curl into a frown as minutes go by and she can't make out any of their words.

A huge crash of metal on metal causes her eyes to fly open.

"Woah, that was heavier than I thought it would be." The low voice sounds above the ringing of the metal.

"Yeah, you need some serious muscles to lift them. But I thought everyone used cast-iron around here," the granddaughter says.

"Nah, I don't own a cast-iron pan. I don't do much cooking, honestly."

"My mom switched to cast-iron when we were growing up, and they took a long time for me to get strong enough to lift, but I prefer them now."

The ringing stops, and the voices drop back to a quieter pitch that June can no longer hear. But that doesn't bother her at all. She has an idea. Not just any idea. A brilliant idea.

Sliding her phone open, she begins carrying out her not-fully-formulated plan.

20

BROOKE

Beck left after a lunch of grilled ham and cheese sandwiches and tomato soup, and I find myself missing his presence. I'm sitting on my bed, thinking about painting, but I can't seem to muster up the enthusiasm for a landscape right now. Instead, my fingers keep tugging on my hair, and my eyes keep drifting to the window, which doesn't even face Beck's house.

When I snap a pink strand off, I know I need to do something else. I grab the crochet blanket I'm working on, and as I work the hook through the yarn, I think, *Get a grip, girl. It's been one date.*

And yet, it's true: I miss him. He's honestly not the most physically attractive man I've ever met, and he's certainly not the most talkative, but he is different from all of the guys who've taken me out.

Maybe he'd be running for the hills if he knew I heard what he said to Meemaw about marrying me, but he also didn't run for the hills despite Meemaw's threats involving munitions.

Ol' Eddie, my goodness.

"Brookie," Meemaw calls from the couch. "Could you help me? I'm ready for a change of location."

"Sure thing, Meemaw," I shout to ensure she hears that I'm coming and doesn't try to do anything foolish.

The soft pink shag carpet tickles my bare toes as I walk down the hallway, and my eyes snag on the line of photographs spaced evenly on the wall. Everything about Meemaw's house is clean. Faded, yes. Old, definitely, but clean. The photograph of her and her husband on their wedding day stands out in a way that never has before.

Meemaw wears a simple white suit skirt and hat, while Pappaw wears company overalls.

Meemaw calls for me again, breaking me from studying the photo.

I shake my head as I try to come back to the present.

"Coming!" I yell.

I plod down the hallway to the living room, trying to formulate the questions I have about that picture, but they're all jumbled up.

Why did it never occur to me to ask Meemaw about her marriage?

"What took you so long?" Meemaw asks. "I have a hankering to be on my porch right now with a glass of lemonade, and my demanding neighbor"—she winks—"insists I can't walk myself out there." She points to her walking boot.

I smile because she's playing up the *her neighbor* angle for a reason, and I suspect I'm about to find out why. An afternoon porch talk with a glass of lemonade might be just the thing to help me figure out whatever I'm feeling about Beck.

Why do I like him so much after one date? And one that, honestly, wasn't ideal?

I mean, his ex-fiancée who left him at the altar showed up. That's not exactly a cute first-date story. Certainly not a story I want shared at my wedding.

Wait, what? Now I'm imagining getting married to Beck. Can someone *please* slow my brain down?

I help Meemaw up, and with the knee scooter Beck brought for her, I stabilize her and assist her out to the porch. We awkwardly maneuver to the old, creaky porch swing in the corner. Once she's seated, I dash back to the kitchen and return with a pitcher of lemonade and two glasses. When I've poured both glasses and settled on the porch swing beside her, Meemaw turns her gaze away from the road and fixes me with her blue eyes.

"What's on your mind, honey?"

Did Mom say we weren't sure if Meemaw was losing her faculties? Because this woman is alert and mischievous, but in the best possible way.

I find I can't look her in the eye for long. Her gaze is too intense. It's like she can read my thoughts. Maybe she can—I've always had an overly expressive face.

"I like him a lot, and that's scary," I mutter to the wide planks of the porch.

"Why is liking a handsome, attractive, successful man scary?" Meemaw's leathery hand grasps mine, and I look back at her worn and weathered face.

"Because I like him a lot. And it was only one date, and I wasn't even sure why he was asking me out. You know? Did he only ask me out because you told him to, and he has some sort of Southern manners toward older women that makes him do what you say even if he didn't want to?"

"Brooke." She tilts her head to the side. "There is no man on the planet who would want to ask you on a date because of what I say. Beckett just needs some pushing."

"But why should he need pushing?"

"I think you know that already. All that rigamarole with what's-her-name—"

"Addie," I supply

"Addie. Yes, that was it."

"I ... uh ... I met her today."

Meemaw's eyes widen, and she blinks slowly. "And you are just *now* telling me you met the *other woman*?"

I bristle at the salacious phrase. "This isn't a soap opera, Meemaw."

She huffs, but the twinkle in her eye tells me she knows exactly what she's doing.

I blow out a breath in the hope of finding the courage for the question I really want to ask.

"What is it, Brooke?" She squeezes my hand gently. "You can ask or tell me anything. And if it involves hanky-panky with the good doctor, I'll just call the church ladies up and get you two down the aisle. He's Catholic, but he was willing to marry Addie at the Baptist church, so no need to worry."

I start to retort about how fast that would be for 'hanky-panky,' but stop when I see the teasing light in her eyes. As usual, my meemaw has disarmed me. She might be eccentric, but she's my grandmother, and I love her dearly.

"How did you know Pappaw was the one?"

"Ah." Meemaw quirks her head to the side, and her gray chignon bobs as she reads my face like one reads a book. "You've moved on from thinking of happily ever afters are guaranteed and are now hopeless about love?"

I shrug. "Yes. Maybe? I don't know if I'm hopeless right now."

"But you were?"

"Maybe. I think..." I scrunch my eyes closed and admit the truth. "I think I'm scared."

"Sweetie. Love is a lot of things—attraction, sure, but mostly it's a choice. Willing the good of the other and finding someone who wills your good. When you both want what's best for the other and are willing to sacrifice your own happiness for them, that's when you know."

"But how did you know?"

"Well, Johnny and I didn't know each other long. We tended to rush into things back then. Maybe it's just all youth who do that, but it was a different time. We got married on a Tuesday, because that was the only time Johnny's supervisor would let him off early. I knew when he came to the house to ask my daddy if he could take me for a soda that this was a different kind of man. And in those days, the men weren't always so manly as to own up to their actions. Maybe this will shock you, but I was pregnant. Johnny didn't care that some man had tried to ruin my life. I was stubborn enough to not let that scum ruin it, mind you."

"Mom?" I ask, surprised to hear that Pappaw wasn't my biological grandfather.

"No, honey, another baby that was adopted by a good family in that county. Johnny and I left the area and came here after that. Too much pain for me there. Sweetie, not many men would look at a woman back then who was unwed and with child, but Johnny saw me call that man out at a dance, and he liked my spirit. He made it his mission to provide for me, and if I hadn't felt adoption was the right choice for that baby, he would have cared for him too."

"Does Mom know?" I ask. She's never mentioned anything about a brother.

"I'm not sure, sweetie. We didn't talk about it much. Now, though, that I'm older, I wish I had." She sips her lemonade, then puts the glass down on the table next to the swing. "The point is, good men exist, and good men are worth it. And I've met more than my fair share of the bad ones. So you go ahead and get to know"—she adopts a low voice and tries to make herself sound like our next-door neighbor—"Doctor Beckett Whistler. He's a good man, and that shouldn't scare you. That should thrill you."

21

BECK

I've had hard nights at work before, but last night takes the cake. My fingers cramp as I grip the steering wheel and take the turn into the driveway. I couldn't spend a single second more at the hospital, so I forewent my usual shower. I don't know if day shifts will be easier, and while I don't put any stock into the old 'full moon' theory of crazy behavior, at least when I finally move to days, I won't have to deal with men who climb on top of their vehicles to howl at the full moon after too many adult beverages, and then fall off said vehicle. Which results in a trip to the E.R., where I get to check for concussions and broken bones and discover that their BAC is 0.24%.

The truth is that some days, I'm just *done*. Some days, I wonder why I didn't choose a safer career, like being an accountant. Sitting quietly behind a computer screen all day—ruining my eyes slowly, to be sure, but ruining them *quietly*. That sounds like a dream right now.

My day off is tomorrow, and I'm relieved. When I'm hanging on by a thread and about to drop off over the cliff of burnout, a day off is exactly what this doctor ordered. I know I need good sleep, a warm meal, and lots of rest.

I mentally flip through the next twenty-four hours. Since tomorrow is Sunday, I'll be able to attend Mass at my favorite church. Although I go every week, I have to vary where I go based on my work schedule.

I blow out a breath. Rest and Mass together make for a perfect weekend.

My eyes involuntarily track to June's house. I think June is Methodist, but I have no idea if Brooke practices faith. I'd like to know that, but I don't know if I can ask her outright. I do know that there is one way to find out, and it involves the little old church ladies my grandma is friends with. Those women have a better secret communication system than the U.S. Armed Forces during a war. It baffles me how they know everything about everyone. It is not uncommon for one of them to call me up after a particularly difficult shift and ask me *how* so-and-so is doing after seeing me in the E.R. last night.

I never divulge patient information—because I would prefer to not get sued for malpractice and breach of contract and a million other things—but the fact that they *know* is enough to be disconcerting.

A flash of pink catches my vision as I veer into my part of the driveway, leaving the shared portion behind. Brooke straightens to her full height from where she was crouching down by my ancient front door.

A smile flits over her face as she sees me and tosses her hair over her shoulder. I throw the truck into park and hop out.

"Hey," she says, walking toward me.

"Hi," I mutter, unsure of what she could possibly have been doing on my porch. My expression must give me away because she quirks her brow.

"Meemaw sent me over. She insisted I drop off a tray of fried chicken for you." She drops her voice to a whisper. "She sat on a chair in the kitchen and heckled me the entire time I was making it."

"You made it?" I ask, already looking around for the tray of chicken and trying to catch a whiff of the lingering scent in the air. There isn't any smell, and as I look over the railing of my porch, there isn't anything on the porch either. "Where is it?"

Brooke looks at the ground. "Meemaw told me to use the spare key to put it on warm in your oven."

I did give June a spare key when I was näive and neighborly with her when I first moved in. I'm not worried about physical safety when it comes to June having access to my house; it's more the principle of the thing. Annoyed at myself for giving June a key and also annoyed at not being annoyed that Brooke was in my house without my knowledge, I have to ask the question. "What were you doing when I came up the driveway? I'm not stupid enough to keep a key under my welcome mat."

Brooke tips her head to the side. "I dropped the key. I was picking it up, and I found this." She holds out a small envelope with my name handwritten on it. "I didn't open it, but it was kind of stuck in between the floorboards of your porch, and I had to jimmy it out of the crack."

I take the envelope, staring at the old-time cursive script that simply says 'Beckett.' The envelope is white but mottled with yellow spots, so I can't tell how long it's been on the porch.

Because I don't have all my faculties after that shift, I ask the dumbest question I possibly can in the moment as I stare at the envelope. "Who's it from?"

Brooke blinks at me and shrugs. "I have no idea." She takes in my haggard appearance. "The chicken is in the oven on warm, and you look like you need a nap."

She walks away, and suddenly I have no desire to do anything but throw the envelope back into the depths of my porch and invite her in for fried chicken. Is it weird she left it in my house? Yes. Is it weird that I want to go eat it and let her see how much it means to me to have hot food ready after last night? Also yes. But I'm past caring.

Just as I'm about to call her back, I catch a whiff of my own body odor. I smell like antiseptic and fried onions.

I almost don't even care about that, but in my indecision, I tear a corner of the envelope and see the sort of kitschy art of spoons and a mixing bowl that belong on a recipe card. My curiosity piqued, I open the envelope and pull out what is, in fact, a recipe card.

It takes some time, but I am able to decipher the title of the card. *Neighborly Fried Chicken*

I flip the card over and find a handwritten note. *"Neighbor, since food is meant to be shared, I'll pass this recipe along to you. Know I'll make it for you anytime because I could use the company, but you can make it yourself too. Maybe even impress a woman with it. -June MacCord."*

Instantly, my eyes burn. I've been so annoyed with June, thinking she was crafty with her chicken trick when I first moved in. Turns out, she genuinely wanted to do something nice for me. And in a place where family recipes are often more highly guarded than the Treasury Department, she gave hers away.

And I, the awkward man that I am, have never once asked her to make it for me again.

I resolve right then and there to make it up to June. Starting with eating the chicken she made Brooke make for me.

All this time, I thought I was alone after Addie, but June's been there looking out for me. She's done it a different way than I would have preferred, but she's cared just the same.

I whistle as I walk into my house and let the smell of burned chicken assault my nose.

It would appear that Brooke might be an expert in fried chicken under June's tutelage, but she is not an expert in ovens because she set mine to broil, not warm. A few minutes more, and the entire house might have gone up in flames.

I dispose of the charred chicken quickly, and when I'm done, I pick up June's recipe card. I know exactly what I'm doing after I shower and sleep.

22

BROOKE

Meemaw's sprained ankle healed over the last week, which means she can use her knee scooter more reliably. Beck's stern chat with her about *not* using it as a step ladder seems to have sunk in, because we haven't had any incidents. Truthfully, I'm a little bored just being at the house with Meemaw all day when she's listening to the doctors and resting.

Beck stopped by for lemonade on the porch swing once this week, but he's been busy. I know when I see his truck in the driveway that he's sleeping because he hasn't switched to day shifts yet.

Ben repaired Meemaw's old car, and I can drive again, but there aren't a lot of things for me to do around here other than hike, and while hiking can be a great solitary activity, I need interactions with *people*. I'm an extrovert, and I wear the title proudly.

My toes push against the faded boards of the porch, starting the swing into motion as I stare at Beck's truck. It's two p.m., and I know he worked last night, so he's still sleeping. It doesn't stop me from wishing I had someone to talk to.

I pull out my phone. Lizzy texted me late last night, but she's in school now.

OMG! He asked Lara. Thank you so much, Brooke! You're my favorite big sister.

I can only assume she means that Joey asked Lara, but if he did, I had nothing to do with it.

I contemplate calling Matt, but decide against it. The only thing I could tell him about here is Beck, and I do not want to talk about boys with my twin brother.

I scroll through my contacts, hoping to find someone I actually want to and can talk to. I stop at the P's. It's been a while since I've talked with Paige. She's been busy with her life as a married woman, but if anyone knows about a man who's hung up on another woman's rejection, it would be her.

I click the text icon because I'm not a terrible friend, and I know that you simply always text first.

Hey, so I'm in West Virginia with my grand-ma, and there's a guy

My thumb accidentally hits send before I can finish my message.

I'm in the middle of typing *Who kind of has a history a lot like Connor's* when my phone rings.

I slide the bar to accept the call, and as I bring the phone up to my ear, I hear Paige's voice.

"There's a *guy*? In West Virginia?"

"Uh. Hi to you too, Paige."

"Nope. We are well past formalities here. I need the details."

I sigh and settle into the porch swing. "My meemaw's neighbor is the guy."

"Ok. And?"

"He was left at the altar by his fiancée years ago."

"Ouch."

"I thought maybe, I don't know, maybe you might have some advice because of everything with Connor."

"I don't know that I have advice, but I can tell you that it's hard when someone has a rejection wound."

"But clearly she wasn't right for him anyway though. Also ... I ... uh ... I met her."

Paige is silent.

"And uh ... she wasn't very nice. I don't know ... it just. The whole thing was weird. I met her on my first date with Beck."

"Ooooh. Beck. I like this name. Well, he got over it enough to ask you out. Did he ask you out again?"

"Kind of. Sort of. It's just—we have to go slow. I guess she hadn't been here since their wedding day, and then she showed up, and it was just ... a lot."

"Well, I don't know if this Beck is the one for you, but if he is, then it's worth going slow, and it's worth the struggle."

"That sounds entirely too reasonable. All I want to do is kiss the man, and that hasn't happened yet."

Paige's voice sounds away from the phone like she's talking to someone else. I make out the words "I'm talking to Brooke" before a deeper voice joins the phone conversation.

"Hey, Brooke, you're *not* keeping Matt in line right now? Then *who is?*"

I laugh. "Hey, Connor. Matt has a serious girlfriend these days. He's grown up a lot since that summer at CGO."

"Oh, so I can't tap him to be a counselor again?"

"You don't work there anymore."

"Hey, it is Paige's and my turn to be there this summer supporting Tom and Lois and the whole crew of campers."

"Yeah, yeah. Could I speak with your wife again, *please*?"

Paige giggles, and I have no idea what marital intimacy just took place off-screen, but I'm simultaneously glad I couldn't see it and also pricked with jealousy because I want *that*. I want a spouse sneaking kisses, or tickling me, or just being affectionate with me, no matter what.

"So you're in West Virginia?" Paige says, just the slightest bit breathless.

"Yes, and now that Meemaw's doing better, I'm—" I drop my voice to the barest of whispers because I do not want Meemaw to overhear what I'm about to say. "I'm bored out of my mind."

"You need your people time," Paige responds. The summer we were camp counselors together led us to know each other in a way that's more like siblings than friends. She absolutely knows I need time with people, the same way I know she needs time *away* from people. "You should get a job."

I blink slowly. A job sounds perfect. I haven't wanted to figure out anything for employment because I didn't know how long I'd be here, but there's nothing for me in Marquette right now, and I might as well have a little money coming in. Surely Meemaw won't mind if I'm gone a few hours a week.

"Brooke?" Paige asks, concern in her voice.

I shake myself out of my stupor. "What? Sorry. A job sounds like a great idea. Why didn't I think of that?"

"I have no idea, but I will take credit for being a genius."

"Fine. Paige, you're a genius," I deadpan. "Now, could you tell me about how being married is treating you these days?"

She lets out a happy hum. "It's amazing. We have an adventure week planned soon. I'm really excited about it."

"What's an adventure week?" I ask.

"It's a week off, and we're going somewhere, but we just don't know yet. We'll see where the road takes us."

I'm grateful Paige cannot see my face through the audio-only phone call because it has landed on an expression of supreme disgust. Not planning a trip? That sounds terrible.

"Sounds … not planned."

It's comical how I can envision her bristling on the other end of the line.

"Connor likes the spontaneity of it. I do too."

I laugh, energized by a conversation with a friend. "Well, New River Gorge is a great place to visit if you're so inclined."

"I'll do some—" she cuts off. "Oh, sorry, Brooke, but I gotta go. Let me know how things go with the neighbor. I'll pray for you."

"Bye, Paige."

I smile. Paige has changed so much since I first met her almost three years ago. The way she naturally doles out the promise of prayer is a far cry from the woman who didn't have faith at camp.

I click the internet icon and start humming to myself as I begin my job search.

23

BECK

Brooke likes June's porch swing. And somewhat foolishly, I look for her on it every time I am coming or going from my house. I'm glad I braved the naked old men at the gym facility attached to the hospital after my lengthy E.R. shift, because today I do not smell like antiseptic and fried onions. I'm doubly glad because, as I pull into the shared portion of my and June's driveway, my eyes track to June's porch swing, where Brooke sits.

Brooke sees me, hops up, and waves. It almost looks like she's waving me over, but I can't tell for sure.

I roll down the window, and she runs down the porch steps and to my truck.

I guess she did want to see me.

"Hey, Beck!" she says through a slightly labored breath. "I know you're busy, but could you help me with something?"

"Sure," I say, my eyes tracking to her lips as she bites the bottom one, but what I really mean is, *Absolutely, I'll help you with anything. Is it by chance mouth-to-mouth resuscitation?*

"I'm looking for a job, but I can't figure out what's a good place to work around here."

"Oh." My shoulders deflate. She wants me to help her find a job. A job means she won't be sitting on June's porch swing all the time. I really like her on that porch swing.

"It's just that I'm here for a while, and Meemaw's doing better, so I need something to do."

My mind glitches. She's here for a while. Of course she should find a job. Maybe a job she loves so much she'll stay forever.

"Tourist season is winding down, but maybe Logan will know something," I suggest. "Or maybe Ben?"

"Would you ask? I need something to do." Her fingers grip the side of my car over the window, and she looks conspiratorially from side to side. "I'm losing my mind."

"I would have thought that taking care of June was a full-time job," I drawl.

Brooke beams at my joke as she tucks the one pink strand of hair that always seems to be escaping from her ponytail behind her ear. The woman actually understands my humor.

"It can be, but we both need a little space. She's used to her quiet time, and by quiet time, I mean time to watch her soap opera shows without me around."

"I thought her favorite show was *Beverly Hillbillies*."

"Oh, it is," Brooke says as she absentmindedly fingers the ponytail resting over her shoulder. "But I like that one too, so she doesn't have to watch it alone."

"Is that why you're always on the porch swing?" I ask.

She flushes a light pink in return. "No…" She doesn't look me in the eye. "I just like the porch swing. Nice…scenery out here and all."

The way she doesn't meet my gaze directly makes me think that maybe she's on the swing because she's looking for me. A thrill works its way up my heart, and never mind the fact that it's eight in the morning and I'm exhausted after a long shift.

I turn the truck off. "I can help you look for something now, if you'd like."

Brooke's smile seems to have the same effect on me as straight caffeine. My heart beats a little faster, and suddenly, I'm wide awake.

Brooke steps back as I open the door and start walking to June's porch along with her.

"So what do you want to do?" I ask.

Her brow furrows in confusion. "What do you mean?"

"What sort of job do you want? What things do you like to do?"

"Oh," she breathes. "I enjoy painting, but that's not really something I want to do for money, and also, I don't know, just something fun where I can be around people a few hours a week."

By now, we've reached June's porch swing, the white paint on the slats chipping a little after years of exposure to mountain air. Still, the pillows on the swing make it comfortable, and I hold the swing steady as Brooke sits down. When I sit down, she tucks her legs up under her, and I use my own to start the swing in motion.

"You want to interact with people?" I ask after a moment of silence.

"Definitely." She nods. "I can't help it. I'm an extrovert."

That makes exactly one of us.

I pull my phone out of my pocket and fire off two texts. First to Logan, then to Ben.

Beck

Brooke is looking for a job. Got anything she could do part-time?

Ben's response is instantaneous.

Ben

Helping her put down some roots? I can always use another mechanic.

I look over at Brooke, who's eyeing my phone suspiciously. "You aren't by chance a certified mechanic, are you?"

"Nope. I didn't know what to do when the gas tank fell out."

I smile to myself, because she really didn't, and I liked getting to rescue her. "Ben is looking for another mechanic, but that doesn't seem like a good fit."

"Probably not. Unless people want cars they can't drive. Actually, are there any rage rooms around here? Maybe I could open one up."

"Rage room?" I ask, my mind shuffling through images of things like a deck of cards but not landing on anything that makes sense.

"You know, a place people go and break stuff in order to calm down. They're all the *rage*." She elbows my side and wiggles her eyebrows.

I do not laugh. Instead, I fix her with a stern gaze. "Did you just make a dad joke?"

"Low-hanging fruit," she responds. "Too tempting not to try it out. I can tell that was not your style, though, so I'll refrain in the future."

I don't know what to say to this woman who is so naturally herself around me. A bit of an enigma, but one I'm enjoying puzzling out. I study her face, and that scar on her left eye catches my gaze. My hand reaches out, and I trace the line with my forefinger as she sits perfectly still at my contact.

"What happened?" I ask in a voice far more gravelly than normal.

Her blue eyes widen, and her lips part slightly, and I think she might lean in to kiss me—but then my phone buzzes and breaks the moment.

She sits back abruptly, and I look down at the phone on my lap to hide my disappointment.

Logan

We need someone to do reservation check-ins for the rafting groups twice a week.

I take a moment to collect myself and paste on a smile even though I really wish we weren't interrupted.

"Good news," I say with forced cheer. "Logan says they need someone to help with the reservations for rafting groups twice a week."

"Oh, wow. That's perfect!"

"I'll give him your number and you can talk to him about it."

"Ok. Is there an application?"

"Logan's family owns the rafting company, so probably not, but you can ask him." The words are as dry as sand in my mouth. I hate the idea of giving her information to Logan, but I also know he's my friend, and even if he's a serial dater, he's a good person.

But still, jealousy doesn't taste good.

I click through my contacts and share Brooke Bastion's contact information with Logan. I know this is the normal and right thing to do in this situation, but Logan is also an extrovert, and Brooke might like him more than me. The two of them together would make an unstoppable force.

The jealous part of me ignites. It's hard not to wonder if Logan will be more attractive to Brooke when Logan never lacks dates. Women flock to the man.

Brooke's phone vibrates, and she pulls it from her pocket. "Oh that's perfect!" she says, turning her bright smile on me. "Thank you so much! I start tomorrow. Logan said if you vouched for me, I'm good."

I force a smile back at her obvious enthusiasm even though that means she won't be sitting on June's porch swing and waving to me when I leave for work tomorrow.

"Hmm." She jumps up off the swing and scrolls on her phone for a minute, then begins talking to herself. "I have sturdy shoes, and I have a water bottle, but I don't have a headlamp."

"I do," I blurt.

She blinks at me.

"I have a headlamp. You could use it."

"Oh, that would be great. Logan said the back room gets dark when grabbing supplies and things."

I nod, but a huge yawn escapes me.

"I should go tell Meemaw about my job, and you should probably…" She tilts her head, indicating my house.

I push myself off the porch swing, the one hundred yards between mine and June's house feeling like it might as well be a marathon at this point.

"Hey, Beck."

I turn and look at her.

"Thank you."

"Anytime," I say.

I start to descend the steps when Brooke's arms wrap around my waist in an awkward hug from behind. She lets go quickly before I can turn around and hug her back the way my body craves.

I give a neighborly wave as I trudge the distance between our houses. The first thing I do when I make it inside my front door is text Logan.

Beck

You don't need to hit on Brooke.

Logan's response comes back less than a minute later. It's a GIF of *Lady and the Tramp* eating the impossibly long spaghetti noodle that leads to their dog version of a kiss.

I want to tell Logan to keep his distance, but I also know that he'll never let me hear the end of it if I stake a claim. Not that he'll actually do anything when he knows I'm interested in her—he's too good a friend for that.

Whoever said knowledge is power was right. I know I don't need to respond. But that same knowledge doesn't stop me from typing out a terse message.

Logan responds, followed by a winky face emoji.

Sometimes my friends are insufferable, but I also know that *he* knows not to hit on her, and something about that makes me feel just the tiniest bit better as I collapse on my bed.

I fall asleep thinking about that tiny pink line of scar tissue on Brooke's face and how it looks like a paintbrush.

24

BROOKE

Meemaw is thrilled about my job with Logan at the rafting headquarters.

"Brookie Cookie, that's perfect!" she squeals. "And the hours are just right too."

My hours are 8-12 on Monday and Wednesday, so what she really means is my hours are perfect for her to watch her shows in peace. I get it. I have a tendency to voice comments about some of the soap operas, and there's only so much you can do when you've had limited mobility for a while.

It's too early for Beck to be home from his shift, but I need the headlamp for my first day. I don't want to show up unprepared and come across as disorganized. I know that this is temporary, and that I'll likely never see the people who come through for rafting again, but a girl has some pride, and I was raised to do the right thing. In this case, being prepared for work the way your boss told you to be prepared is the right thing.

I open the front door, stepping out into the brisk mountain morning air. I'm not sure if Beck will be home before I have to leave, but it would really help me a lot if he was, and if he would give me that headlamp to borrow.

I lean against the siding of the house and heave out a sigh, thinking of what to do, when something white flutters just off to the side of my vision on the porch swing. Immediately I cover my head and close my eyes. I do not need an overzealous seagull attacking me today.

It takes a moment before I remember I'm not at Camp CGO, and the seagulls here in West Virginia have not attacked me, so I'm probably safe.

I crack open an eye and stare at the porch swing. Something black is there too.

I draw closer to the suspicious objects and find a headlamp pinning down a piece of plain white paper. The paper was folded in half but flipped open in the wind, leading to the flapping and seagull confusion.

I smile as I pick up the light, knowing Beck left it there for me.

I let my eyes rove the note. Beck's handwriting is surprisingly legible for a doctor. I have to laugh as I read what he wrote.

Brooke,

I wanted to make sure you had this for your first day on the job but wasn't sure if I'd be home in time to give it to you. Good luck.

–Beck

The man of few words uses as few words as possible in every scenario, it seems. I don't really mind, because at least it shows he's consistent.

Pocketing the headlamp in my pink hiking bag, along with the rest of my gear for work, I focus on folding the piece of paper into tiny squares like I'm in highschool and this is a note from a boy I want to save. Scratch that—this *is* a note from a boy that I do want to save, but it's not like it was when I was in high school and desperate for my first kiss and the attention I thought it would bring me.

Thinking about how desperate I was for my first kiss brings my mind back to Paige. When I met her, she'd never had a boyfriend, and now she's happily married to a really great guy. It's funny how someone like Paige, who would not have been popular if she had been in high school with me, ended up with the thing I desperately wanted and had thought popularity would bring.

I slide my phone out of my black capris pocket and fire off a text to Paige.

Brooke

> Thinking of you because I'm on my way to work!

A text comes back almost immediately.

Paige

> Where are you working? What happened with the cute neighbor?

Brooke

> I'll 8ll you in later. Here's where I'm working.

I send her the link to Logan's family's rafting company website. New RAFT River Gorge is a five-star rated adventure company with an impressive website that makes it look like this is going to be a lot of fun. At least the pictures of people wearing helmets and holding brightly painted rafting paddles as they career over a rapid make it look fun. I'm not sure if it's as much fun in real life as it is in a still photograph, but the internet presence is reassuring.

I smile to myself as I drive to work.

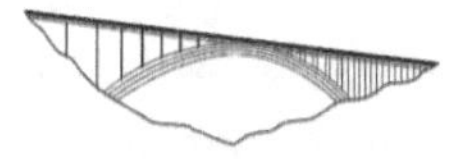

"Hey, hey, new employee." Logan straightens from where he was bent over, securing ropes around a raft, as I approach the front of the open-air rafting check-in stand.

"Hi," I respond, a little breathless from the very steep hike up from the employee parking lot.

A girl who must be Logan's sister steps out from under the shadow of the awning. He mentioned she would be here this morning. "You must be Brooke?"

I nod. "It's so good to meet you! Logan never hires women who aren't family, so it's nice to have a new work friend I'm *not* related to here."

"Lynette," Logan warns.

"Yeah, sure, I know you keep business in the family," Lynette says as she pulls her curly brown hair into a high ponytail and rolls her eyes. She drops her voice to a stage whisper. "Really, he just hits on every woman he meets unless they're related to him, and this is a way to protect the business."

"Lynette!" Logan scolds. Then he looks at me and says, "Sorry, Brooke. Lynette is my younger sister, and she never stops giving me a hard time."

"Well, it's pretty slim pickings for friends around here when you date every woman in my age group who comes through the door."

Logan shrugs. "You wouldn't want to be friends with the tourists anyway."

"So why are you dating them?" she counters.

Logan opens his mouth, then snaps it shut as he fidgets with a knot, clearly uncomfortable. I'm no stranger to sibling banter, but I feel uncomfortable walking into whatever this weird conversation was.

He dusts his hands on his black athletic shorts and then gives his head a shake, but not before he scowls at Lynette. "Well, ignore Lynette, Brooke. I'd fire her, but she's our second-best rafting guide." He sighs. "Let's get you set up."

"Paige?" I call, hardly trusting my eyes. When I turn a little, I find Connor outside the driver door.

"Brooke!" Paige says as she hurries toward me, Connor not far behind.

Logan suddenly appears at my side. "Are these friends of yours?" he drawls.

"I can't believe you're here. So this is where you chose to come on adventure week?" I say to Paige, then turn to Logan. "Logan, this is my friend Paige, and this is Connor. We all worked together a few summers ago at a camp."

"A camp," Logan says as he studies Paige and smiles that blinding smile at her.

Paige brushes a hair off her face, and I spy the glint of her wedding band in the sunlight.

"I take it you're not here to raft?" he asks Connor.

"No, sorry, man. We're here to see Brooke," Connor replies in typical good-natured fashion.

"Eh, that's ok. Rafting's cool, but you have to have reservations." Logan turns back toward me. "I have to head out to meet the group. Great job today, Brooke. Looking forward to having your help from now on."

He waves, and we all wave in return.

"So, Brooke," Connor says, after he plants himself firmly next to Paige and slips an arm around her waist. "What should we do on this adventure?"

"Uh … do you have a place to stay?" I ask.

"Yep! It's only for two nights before we're onto the rest of our adventure. It's the cutest little rental…" Paige looks up at Connor with a tiny blush, and I immediately direct the conversation away from their house because it's clear they love each other very much in private right now, and I'd prefer not to know more about that.

"Great! There's tons of hikes. Rafting, ziplining, rock climbing, fishing, kayaking…" I trail off.

Paige bites her lip and looks unsure for a beat, but it passes quickly.

"Hiking sounds amazing." She leans into Connor. "As long as there are no cougars." She shivers and Connor tightens his arm around her protectively.

"No cougars that I'm aware of," I assure. "The trails can get pretty busy. I think there are bobcats and black bears though."

"That sounds good enough for me. When can we hike?" Connor asks.

"Uh … well, I actually don't really know the trails, but I can ask my neighbor if he'll take us on a hike."

"Oh, the *neighbor*?" Paige asks before letting out a huge yawn. "Sorry, I am absolutely exhausted. We haven't even been to the rental house yet, and we've been on the road since four a.m."

"You guys came right here instead of stopping off and putting your things away?" I ask, shocked.

"Part of adventure week is surprises." Connor shrugs. He knows full well that I do not operate well without planning. My penchant for planning might have been why he hired me to be a counselor at the camp he oversaw. "We wanted to surprise you."

"You definitely did!" I say before giving each of them a hug. "I'm so glad you're here." I take in the circles under Paige's eyes. She really is exhausted. "I think you should head to your house and rest up. I'll ask Beck about hiking tomorrow. It's his day off, so that should be good."

"That sounds great." Connor says, his eyes affectionately fixed on his wife.

"I'll text you once I hear from Beck," I say to the happy couple as we walk toward their car.

Connor holds the door open for Paige, just as he always does.

Paige gives me a quick hug and whispers, "I want to know more about the neighbor next time I see you!"

She climbs into the car. She has to move a well-worn book off the seat before she can sit down, and as she places it on the dashboard, I have to laugh. The woman who claimed she didn't have faith when she started working at Camp CGO just moved a Bible off her seat.

Reflecting on how Paige has changed makes me think two things: One, that I should read my Bible again. And two, that Paige was right. It was worth the struggle and the wait for her. It will be for me too.

With that happy thought, I compose a text to Beck asking if he'll stop by when he's done with work for lemonade on the porch swing.

25

DR. BECKETT WHISTLER

I don't know how Brooke convinced me to lead a group hike with strangers, but they are her friends. Actually, I know exactly how she convinced me. She looked at me with big blue eyes as we sat on June's porch swing and tensed up and started to run her fingers through her hair. When she stopped and clasped both her hands in her lap, she asked me with a *please* that was quiet, not wheedling. A strand of pink hair lifted off her neck in the breeze, and I knew I'd do anything she asked.

Connor is chatty, which might annoy me, but seems to be fun for Brooke, who returns his banter good-naturedly. From what I've gathered, the three of them all worked at a summer camp, and that's where Connor fell for Paige. I'm used to being a silent observer, and that's exactly the role I've fallen into with this group.

"I need a minute," Paige calls out. We all stop and turn back to look at Paige. She's got one hand over her stomach like she has a cramp, and she looks pale. "You guys go up ahead. I'll catch up."

Brooke and Connor start walking again, but some internal doctor sense tells me to check on Paige. When I look back at where Paige was standing, I see that she's disappeared into the brush alongside the trail. I wait for a moment in case she's using the bathroom, but then I hear the unmistakable sound of someone retching.

"Paige?" I call quietly. The shuffling of feet on brambles tells me which direction she went. "Paige, I'm a doctor. Are you ok?" I push some growth aside and find her kneeling on the ground, clutching her stomach.

"Yeah, I just…"

Maybe it's not the first thing everyone thinks of when they see a woman who's vomiting on the side of a trail, but I've been a doctor for years. If there is one thing I've learned, it's that you always rule out pregnancy.

"Paige." I crouch next to her and look her in the eyes. "Are you pregnant?"

Paige's eyes meet mine with a soft light as she nods her head in a yes.

"Does Connor know?"

"Not yet. I'm not very far along, but I've been sick the past few days. I wanted to make it to my first appointment next week to tell him."

I tip my head to the side, confused. "Why would you wait to tell him?"

She sighs. "He loves kids, and we've been trying for over a year, and it hasn't happened yet, and he's been so disappointed. He never says anything, but I can tell."

I've known Brooke's friends for less than two hours at this point, but it's clear as day that the man is devoted to his wife. His personality is exactly the opposite of mine, and he uses nine times as many words in a minute as I do, but he'd want to know.

I put my hand on her arm. "Paige, you need to tell him."

"But what if I mess it up?" she whispers just barely above the breeze. "What if I lose the baby?"

I frown. Counseling emotional women is not something I'm equipped to do, but Paige is looking at me with vulnerability, and I can't not say anything to her.

"There's nothing you can do to mess it up. I can't tell you why miscarriages happen, or why they are so common, but I think Connor would want to know. You don't have to be alone in the earliest part of pregnancy just because society says you shouldn't tell people."

Paige stands on shaky legs, brushing leaves and detritus off her shorts. "Thanks." She reaches into her small hiking backpack and extracts a water bottle. She takes a sip, then grimaces and clutches her stomach again.

I pull my backpack off and open up the front zippered pocket. I like the taste of ginger better than breath mints, so I always carry hard ginger candies.

"Here," I say, holding out the ginger candies. "Ginger helps settle the stomach."

"Thanks." She takes the candies, unwraps one, and pops it into her mouth. "Do you..." She checks over her shoulder before scrunching her eyes shut, then whispering, "Do you think I could tell Connor someplace private?"

Finally, a patient who's listening to me!

Paige reminds me of myself. She's more quiet and reserved.

"Yes. There's an outlook up ahead, and Brooke and I will leave you two alone for a bit."

"Paige? Are you ok?" Connor's voice sounds from on the trail, laced with worry.

"Y-yeah. Just needed a minute," she calls back.

I lead the way back to the trail, with Paige following. Connor eyes me with suspicion, but then turns his attention back to his wife.

Strands of Brooke's pink hair have escaped her braid and are blowing around her face as she waits behind Connor.

"Beck?" she questions. "What's going on?"

"Just checking on her. She's ok."

"Yeah. Well, it's weird that you went to check on her when she was using the bathroom," Brooke says, and I don't miss the hint of jealousy in her voice.

I slide my hand over Brooke's. "I can't tell you more, but I promise you, checking on her was the right thing to do." I look back at Connor and Paige. Connor's arm is wrapped possessively around Paige's waist as he glares at me. I shake my head and am about to tell him, "Dude, I'm a doctor," but bite my tongue. I suspect Connor's whole outlook on life is about to change in a very big way.

"Everyone ready?" I call, mostly talking to Paige. She gives a subtle nod and a tight-lipped smile. With that reassurance, I start us off down the trail again.

It's a quarter mile before we come to the first overlook off the trail. Paige and Connor have fallen a bit behind, so I stop and wait for them next to the side trail. Brooke starts to head down it, but I put my hand out on her arm to stop her. Her brow furrows.

Paige and Connor approach, so I drop my voice. "Let's let the two of them experience this one alone, ok?"

"What is with you?" Brooke hisses.

"Please, just trust me," I whisper as Connor stops short next to me, Paige's hand tucked in his. I meet Paige's eyes and tip my head toward the side trail. "We'll give you some time to enjoy the view together," I say in my regular voice.

Connor's face flashes confusion, but Paige tugs him down the trail to the overlook.

They disappear down the side trail, and Brooke crosses her arms over her chest. "What. Are. You. Doing?"

"C'mon," I say, touching Brooke's arm. "I can't tell you, but I think you'll find out soon. We can wait for a while. They need some time."

"Beck." Brooke's voice is full of derision. "This is really weird."

I know I have a good reason for this, but there's nothing else I can say, so I shrug. I spy a fallen log a few yards up the trail and stalk over to it. I sink onto the log, removing my backpack in the process. Brooke follows suit.

Just as she starts to lower onto the log, we hear the unmistakable sound of Connor's shout.

Brooke springs up, ready to run. Her eyes flit to my face for a second, where I lean back on my hands, completely unresponsive to the commotion.

"Beck! What if they need help? What if Paige has fallen off the cliff?" She takes off running, and I have no choice but to follow her even though I really don't want to interrupt their private moment.

26

BROOKE

Why is Beck being so strange? Why isn't he concerned? All the *why* questions ricochet in my mind as I burst through the brush and onto the overlook.

I stop short.

I'm greeted by the sight of Connor, his arms around Paige, her arms clasped around his neck, and her feet slightly off the ground as he kisses her.

"Really?" he asks, pulling back, his mouth agape as he places a hand on Paige's stomach. It hits me then. She's pregnant. And he didn't know.

"Really," Paige says in reply, and Connor kisses her again.

In mortification at my near interruption, I start to back away, to let them have this time together.

"I told you to let them have their private moment." Beck's voice sounds from right next to my ear.

"What?" I turn toward Beck, and he's closer than he's ever been of his own accord. My eyes flit to his lips for a beat. It would be so easy to turn and kiss him. But Beck takes a step back and leaves distance between us.

When my gaze lands on Connor and Paige again, I find that although they could be looking out at the beautiful view of the New River below, their eyes are fixed on each other.

"Congratulations, man," Beck says to Connor, extending his hand.

Confusion flashes across Connor's face, but then he smiles. "You knew?"

Beck shrugs. "I'm an E.R. doctor. We rule pregnancy out first thing, always."

Connor grasps Beck's hand and gives it a hearty shake. "I can't believe it. I'm going to be a dad." He turns toward Paige, and the look on his face is so full of awestruck love that I experience a punch to the gut with how beautiful it is. *With how much I want that.*

I want someone to look at me the way Connor looks at Paige *right now*. And believe me, I have seen Connor look at Paige—an entire summer of the two of them pining after each other will do that—but there is something different in this moment.

A pang of sadness crosses through my body, and loneliness floods my very soul. Happy for Paige and Connor, yes, but sad for me. Sad for my woeful experiences with dating and staying true to my values, and sad that the man I'm interested in right now has such a huge hang-up in his past that things have to move slower than molasses in a Marquette January.

I turn away from the happy couple, and my eyes find Beck. He's not looking at Paige and Connor, he's looking at me. There's a tenderness in his smile that I haven't seen before. I'm tempted to ask him what he's thinking, but then he quirks his eyebrow and says, "Better tell June. I'm sure she'll have something to say about the happy news."

I blow out a breath, trying to expel the longing from my body. "Yeah, she'll probably get right on knitting a blanket as she asks me when I'll be giving her a great-grandchild."

I step around Beck and start back up the trail, but the crunch of feet on leaves behind me tells me that he followed. "So," he says.

I turn and face him. "So?"

"So, do you want kids?" he asks point-blank.

I blink. "Uh. Yeah."

"Hmm." Beck offers nothing else. He remains silent, so I turn away from him and begin walking. Again, he follows. Again, not saying anything. I know he doesn't talk a lot. I know he has a hard time thinking about the future with everything that happened with Addie, but right now, I'm emotionally shredded. I like Beck, but if the outcome of dating a man isn't the look of pure love and joy that I witnessed on Connor's face just now, then *what* is the point of attraction?

Tears spring to my eyes, unbidden, and I pretend to cough so I can wipe them away without Beck seeing.

"Brooke?" Beck's hand grasps my elbow, and he brings it gently down away from my face. "Why are you crying?" The rough pad of his other hand's thumb swipes a tear off my cheek, and I can't stop the words as they come bubbling out.

"Because I want *that*." I point down the trail to where Paige and Connor are busy celebrating their joyful news. "I want to find love. And I haven't found it yet, and every time I go out with a man, I find out they just want one thing, and it's..." I close my eyes at the implication before continuing. "And maybe I'm just too much for guys. I know my personality is big and that I take charge, and maybe men don't like that, but I can't change who I am. And I do want to be a mom one day. And it's just..." I blow out a shaky breath.

Beck's hand stills on my elbow, his warmth seeping into my skin. "It's just what?" he asks, his voice rough.

I stare at the ground when I answer. "It's just seeming less and less likely that I'll ever find someone."

I bite my lip as I look at him.

His brown eyes meet mine in a serious, piercing gaze.

"Brooke…" Beck begins, but I hold a hand up and interrupt him.

"No, Beck, I understand. You have a lot of things to work through, and dating isn't going to be normal for you—but I don't know what that even means. I just know that at the end of my life, I want there to be a whole gaggle of grown children and their gaggles of little children around me while I accidentally spit my dentures out when I blow out the candles on my one-hundredth birthday cake."

In frustration, I wipe the rest of the tears away with my sleeve with more force than necessary.

Beck's large hand lands on my other elbow, and he turns me toward him. He steps closer, his eyes locked on mine. "Brooke," he whispers, his voice cracking slightly. "You'll have that." And then his lips brush my forehead. "Be patient with me?"

I've never met anyone like Beck, and the physical attraction is there, but more than that, there's a brokenness he allows me to see. Paige's words about being patient and the struggle being worth it ring in my mind.

My whisper floats on the wind as I let myself believe that Paige is right. Maybe I could have a future that looks like hers. Maybe it's just make-believe. But I have to try.

"Ok."

MEEMAW

June MacCord is not without technological savvy. She has the Facespaces, the TicketyTockies, and the InstantGratification apps all ready to go. What June MacCord does not have, however, is the patience—and time—required to unfreeze the browser when it lags.

A brief wind gust, and suddenly, June MacCord is pressing the "add to cart" button relentlessly. Despite her determination, the number remains stuck at zero.

In frustration, June throws the phone away from her just as her granddaughter and her beau walk through the door.

June's attention leaves the disobedient website and focuses on the couple in front of her. There's something drawn in both of their faces, something that wasn't there before they left.

Alarm bells blare in her mind. "What did you do?" She levels a glare at her neighbor. "Why is my Brooke upset?"

The neighbor sighs as the granddaughter turns to him. "I'll handle it. I'm fine. Really." The young man looks as if he doesn't believe her, but he turns to leave anyway.

"Goodbye, Miss June," he calls softly as he steps over the threshold and out of the house.

June turns her attention back to her granddaughter. "Tell me everything." She pats the spot on the faded floral sofa beside her.

The granddaughter sinks into the couch and launches into her tale of dating woes.

June is so engrossed in the tale and consoling her granddaughter that no one notices when the phone sinks into the crack between the cushions and the back of the sofa. And neither of them notices that the "add to cart" button has unfrozen and is now in the hundreds.

June pulls her granddaughter in for a hug, and in the shifting of the couch and weight distribution, the side button to confirm the order has been pressed—twice.

27

BECK

I see tears fairly regularly. Pain does that to people, and people tend to avoid the E.R. unless they are in severe pain. I remain fairly unaffected by it. But now I need to add qualifiers, because I *am* affected by Brooke's tears. Someone that vivacious should not be crying because of hopelessness about men, of all things.

Brooke's dream of spitting out her dentures when she's one hundred, in front of a huge family, is the opposite of what I've thought my dream is. The dream in which I am left alone, unbothered, and honestly, I never considered what would happen when I got older because I'd need people, and I do not want to need anybody.

Brooke's vision has people in it that she loves. How is it possible to imagine loving people you don't even know? People that don't even exist yet, just far-off figments of an idea. It's like that saying older folks are always offering kids when they ask, 'Where was I when some event happened?' and the older people say, "You were just a twinkle in my eye." Was I seeing actual twinkles in Brooke's eyes? I don't know, but something about this is clearly interrupting my typical thought processing.

My hands ball into fists as I walk up the driveway to my house. My lonely house. For so long, my house has been a refuge. A haven of peace after the fast-paced, high-stakes of an E.R. shift, and a place to hide after Addie. Today, the silence feels like a tomb.

Without meaning to, I find myself envisioning Brooke's one-hundredth birthday party. I'm older than her by almost five years, so I'd be well over one hundred if I was there, but if I got to spend the rest of my life knowing Brooke, I'd be a blessed man.

It's that thought that stops me cold. *I'd be blessed to have Brooke in my life.*

I *want* to have Brooke in my life. I want to see her happy and well, and I want to see her have the things she wants. I don't want to see her cry. I want to *give* her the things that she wants.

Oh no. I'm in love.

Two slow-paced, get-to-know-you dates and several porch swing chats later, and I'm in love?

My blood pressure rises. A ringing starts in my ears. This is an emergency. I can't be in love. I don't *do* love.

I pull out my phone and dial the only person I can talk to about this, but my thumb hovers over Brooke Bastion's contact info before scrolling to Ben Painter.

"Hey, man. How was the double date?" Ben's voice drawls through the phone after one ring. He might be obnoxious at times, but he's my best friend.

"It was a baby announcement," I say dryly.

"Uh … congrats? But people around here are going to talk if you aren't married. You know that, right?"

I roll my eyes. "Not my baby."

"Uh…"

"Brooke's friends. Brooke's very married friends. They're the ones having a baby."

"Oh. I didn't realize they were married."

"Why? Wait … was Logan thinking of making a move on Paige?"

I'm met with silence, which I take as a yes.

"Is Logan there right now?"

More silence.

"Hey, buddy," Logan says.

"Well, since you're there, I guess you can hear this too. I have a problem."

"And it's not a baby," Ben interjects.

"No, it's not a baby. It's just—" I scrub a hand down my face. "I don't know if I can talk to you two about it. You wouldn't understand."

"You're in love with Brooke?" Logan asks.

I blink. The other end of the phone is silent except for the suspicious hissing of whispers and what sounds like cash exchanging hands.

"Uh … Beck? Earth to Beck? Are you still there?"

I shake my head before I can respond. "How did you know?"

Ben sighs. "Because we've known you for almost all of your life. And we were friends with you the…" He trails off, as if he's thinking of how to put it delicately. "The last time you were in love."

"I can't be in love. I don't do that. Not anymore, not ever."

"Sure you don't." Logan snorts. "You have no desire whatsoever to have a wife and kids and to come home after a long day of saving lives to someone who actually likes you instead of an empty house."

"I—"

"Nope. You don't want that. You don't want a *honeymoon*." I know him well enough to know he's waggling his eyebrows at that comment. "You don't want someone to stay warm with on cold nights. Nope, you don't want to die lonely and old, and now that you're almost twenty-nine and have enough distance between Addie and are *feeling* things, you could not possibly be experiencing love."

"Fine," I huff. "I think I love her. But I can't."

"My sister." Ben coughs. "Addie," he corrects. "She told me she saw you. And listen, Beck. Addie's here to stay. You can't let the past control your future anymore. Addie wasn't it for you. And as much as I love her, and as much as I've been your friend for our entire lives, it didn't happen. It's time to move on. Maybe she'll move on, too, once she knows you have."

My brow furrows. "What?" I say dryly. "She's the one who moved on. While we were about to get married in front of an entire church of people. I'd say she moved on awful fast comparatively."

Logan clears his throat this time. "Beck, if you don't want to be with Addie again, you'll need to make that abundantly clear."

"Huh?"

"Addie has…" Ben supplies an unhelpful sentence fragment. The reason he trailed off is clear when Addie's voice comes through.

"I thought my ears were ringing," she says, her voice coming closer. "Who are we talking to, boys?"

I can hear the flirtatious tone in her voice, imagine the way she's sashaying her hips as she walks, see her reaching her hand out to flirt with whoever is on the other end of the line, so I do the only thing I can think of.

I hang up and toss my phone on the counter.

Addie is the past. I'm looking toward the future.

I turn around and walk as fast as I can out the door.

28

BROOKE

Meemaw suggests I take a bubble bath and read a book. But not just any book, a *romance* book from her pile of paperbacks with men wearing breeches—and conveniently no shirts—as they sit on a horse, staring at women in long gloves and gowns, with titles like *The Reluctant Duchess of Lovemore Manor* emblazoned across the scene.

"No thanks, Meemaw," I say as I push off the couch. "I think I'll go wash up and go to—"

A knock on the door interrupts me. Meemaw pats my hand before releasing me. The knock sounds again, louder. I open the door just as Beck is about to pound his fist against the wood for a third time.

He stumbles slightly, catching himself on the doorframe.

"Are you ok?" I ask as I look him over. His mouth sets in a thin line, his jaw tight, his forearms tense. They are really nice forearms.

Beck doesn't respond to my question. He just steps closer, over the threshold, and before I can totally understand what's happening, he leans down and places a kiss on my lips.

My eyes bug out in surprise, although this isn't an unwelcome one. He's not demanding, he's not rough. He's just there, his lips touching mine firmly in far-too-brief a moment before he pulls back and meets my gaze with his own.

I blink a few times, unsure what to say and definitely unsure what that was all about.

Beck straightens and takes a step back. "I'm so sorry," he says, his voice scratchy and low. "I…" He rubs his neck. "I'm sorry."

He turns to leave and steps back onto the porch.

Utterly confused, I look back at Meemaw, whose very unsubtle hand gesture indicates I should follow him to the porch.

I step outside, shutting the door behind me.

"Beck?" I call.

He's on the bottom step, but he stops before he slowly turns and looks at me. The uncertainty in his gaze does me in. He looks like that because he kissed me and thinks I didn't want him to. A confident man who saves lives shouldn't look like a wounded puppy, but in this moment, he does.

"I…" A flush floods my cheeks. "I liked that," I whisper.

Something in Beck's entire demeanor changes. He straightens and walks toward me with the confidence that I usually see in him. The kind of confidence that's extremely attractive.

"You liked what, Brooke?" he asks, his voice extra deep.

"I liked it when you kissed me," I whisper as he steps closer.

I take a step toward him, and he closes the distance. His warm hands land on my back as he pulls me into an embrace. His lips land on mine, gentle and soft.

He's warm and kind and good.

When he pulls away, he looks deep into my eyes and says three words that make my heart hammer out a beat in double time.

"I love you."

29

BECK

Why did I just tell Brooke I love her after our first kiss? Because I'm an idiot, but also because I do love her, and I can't deny it, and my dumb friends are right. The moment those words left my mouth, a peace settled deep within my chest. Something true and good and beautiful sprang to life in my heart.

Brooke doesn't say anything, and it's awkward. I start to back away, dropping my hands from the small of her back, when she opens her mouth, then closes it again.

"I … You?" She closes her eyes. "You love me?" She cracks one eye open like she's trying to make sure I don't disappear.

I bend and place a kiss on the corner of her closed eye, on the scar that reminds me of a paintbrush. "Yes," I say, my voice catching. "I do."

"But you told me…" she starts, trailing off again. "You told me to be patient with you."

"I know I did. I was just too stubborn to admit what I was feeling."

"Because of Addie?" she asks.

Addie's name makes me angry, I don't want anything to do with Addie anymore. Never again.

"No," I say, but I know that's a lie. "A little," I amend. "Mostly, you scare me. I tried to wall myself off, and yet, even with all my defenses, you still managed to get through."

"I wasn't trying…" she starts, but I lightly kiss her lips to stop her.

"I know you weren't. And that's what I noticed. You don't have to try for me to notice you. You don't have to do anything other than be you for me to want to be around you. And I don't like people much, so that makes you really special."

"Yeah, but that doesn't mean you *love* me."

"Brooke?" Her pretty blue eyes captivate me. I lower my mouth to hers and kiss her again, deeper this time. "I think I'd be the one who knows when I love someone."

"But—but…" she sputters as I hold her closer.

"Brooke, please trust me." I whisper the plea against her hair. "I love you." I link her hand in mine and walk toward June's porch swing, holding it steady as Brooke settles on it.

I drop onto the seat next to Brooke and place my arm around her shoulders, pulling her closer to me.

Brooke leans into me, and I savor the feel of her under my arm, the rightness about this.

"But why are you telling me *now*?" she presses. The fact that she hasn't said she loves me back has me retreating inward.

What if she doesn't find me worthy? What if she rejects me too?

I don't think I could handle that.

I meet her eyes with my own serious gaze. "Because I saw something with your friends today that made me think about my future."

"Future…" Brooke says. This woman will not make things easy for me.

"A wife, a family, kids, and all the things I thought I didn't want, especially after … everything."

"But you do want those things?"

"I want that life with the right person. I'd rather have none of it if I had to have it with the wrong person. I was so close to being wrong before, but I've been praying, and this feels right."

"Beck, I—"

My phone begins buzzing. It's my day off, but I must have forgotten to turn off the alarm reminding me to get ready for work. I fish it out of my pocket to turn it off, but see that it's Ben calling. That's weird—Ben never calls. He *always* texts first. I'm immediately worried for my friend, so I motion to Brooke that I need to take this call.

I accept the call and launch into doctor mode. "Ben, is everything ok?"

"Beck?" a distinctly feminine voice says. "I'm so glad I *finally* got through to you."

"Addie?" I question, turning to look at Brooke because I don't understand what's happening right now. But Brooke hops off the swing and stands just to my side as she shakes her head and tears form in her eyes.

"I knew it had to do with *her*," Brooke whispers before she turns the doorknob and slams the front door of June's house.

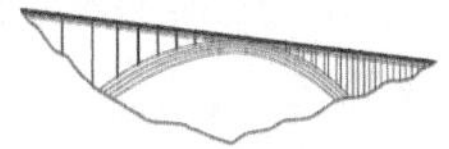

"Addie." I grind her name out through my clenched teeth. "I don't want to talk to you."

"I think you do, Beck," she condescends. "I think you really do."

"I think I really don't," I snap.

She heaves a sigh through the phone. "Listen, Beck. I'm sorry, ok? I wish you could forgive and forget. We were good together."

I snort.

"We were really good together," she continues. "It's just the wedding stuff—it was all too much, and the idea of only ever being with you … well, I had to find out if there was more to the world."

Addie knows how to drive a knife into my heart and twist it. Everything about her apology is about her. I see her so clearly now; it's like scales have fallen from my eyes. I don't want a future with her in it.

"And now that I've explored the world and met other people and saw you with that new girl, it just made me think that we had a good thing, and why would we give it up?"

"You saw me with that new girl?" I question. "Brooke? The woman who was with me when I was at Long Point? That's why you're calling? That's what made you think you should try to get back together with me?" I bark out an incredulous laugh. "How did you convince Ben to let you use his phone?"

"I didn't convince him, I just took it while he was in the shower," she responds. "And come on, Beck. Do you really think her body is better than mine?"

Addie's jealousy is on full display even through the phone, and I can't think of anything more unattractive. My lips curl up in a snarl of disgust. This woman needs to get out of my life. I can't believe I was about to marry her.

"Yes. I do think Brooke is more attractive than you. Don't call me again. I don't want to talk to you."

I hang up the phone and look around the porch for Brooke. Instead of Brooke, I find June leaning on her knee scooter by the front door. June's mouth is set in a thin line, and her eyebrows are drawn up, making sharp carats.

"Young man," she scolds, and it is decidedly not her regular good-natured humor. "You are a fool."

I'm used to being insulted by June, but not when she clearly means it.

I hold my hands out in confusion. "Uh—" I eloquently state.

"No. None of that. You can either be a man, or not. But this *waffling*"—she spits the word at me with the vehemence of a cobra—"will not be something you subject my Brooke to."

"Waff…" I start, but am interrupted by pure fury.

"No." June wags her finger at me while she shakes her head. "I heard enough to know that you are either a stupider specimen of man than most, or you have no regard for people like Brooke. Brooke is kind and honest. She has big dreams, she wants love, and you waltz right on in and dangle the promise of love like a worm on a hook, but when *that woman* calls, you answer. Quite frankly, Brooke is entirely too smart to be with the likes of you."

People do not call doctors stupid, but June doesn't care what people think, what people say. She tells it exactly like she sees it, and I do too. *Brusque* is a word that's been used to describe me a time or two, but it's different when someone else is being brusque with you. Regardless of the social connotations, bluntness can be effective in making someone realize their idiocy.

"June," I say as a weight comes crashing down on my shoulders. I really am stupid. I told Brooke I loved her and then answered the phone. I didn't know it was Addie on the other line, but I still made something else a priority right after declaring love. "I … I'm an idiot."

June shakes her head in agreement.

"Can you help me fix it?"

"No can do, sir. That's all on you." She wheels her scooter back a smidge. "But you better fix it because you and Brooke are meant for each other."

She tosses the words out on the porch before she slams the door, and I'm left staring at the forest-green wood with gold square accents, unsure of how to make everything up to Brooke. But I'm going to try.

30

BROOKE

Baggage is a funny word. I never understood it fully until now. Baggage is when the man who's professing his love to you answers a call from his ex-fiancée instead of letting you finish what you have to say—words that might have sounded a lot like 'I love you too.'

Baggage is thinking you love the man, and being ready to say it, only to be shoved aside for the past.

Meemaw looks up sharply from her phone as I stomp by. I just poured my heart out to her before this, and I don't feel up to pouring it out again. I refuse to meet her gaze as I storm down the hall to my bedroom.

I can't call Paige. I'm not sure how to say, "Hey, friend, so good to see you. I'm super jealous of your life right now, and Beck just said he loved me, but then his ex-fiancée called him, and he answered the phone instead of letting me say I love him back."

I'm about to call Matt in a desperate attempt to find someone to sympathize with me when my phone rings, and it's Beck. I can't talk to him right now. He literally chose Addie over me, so there is no hope of a future with him, even if, for a moment, I had indulged in that dream.

I squash the dream down and reject the call. I know that physically, I can't compete with Addie. She's petite and CoverGirl-perfect. I'm ... not. While I hide them usually, today the tiny cracks in my self-esteem fissure into a full-fledged identity crisis. But that isn't me, and I know it, so I chuck my phone across the room, where it lands face-down on the bright pink shag carpet.

I'm practically vibrating with anger as I stare at that little black rectangle. It's stupid how much power that tiny device has over me, over everyone. I snarl at the phone and then do the only thing I can do when faced with overwhelming emotions: I drop to my knees and reach under the bed to grab the shoebox of paints I brought with me to Meemaw's house.

As I grasp the box, my hand slips and thwacks the carpet under the bed. I slide my hand out to rub the pain away, but a piece of paper catches the corner of my pinky and gives me a paper cut. I'm beyond angry, beyond annoyed, beyond any known human feeling when I pull the paper out, ready to hurl it into the garbage.

The drawing on the paper makes me hesitate. It's a handmade card. Curving along the border are roses and ivy vines, the faint marks of pencil still obvious under the color in a few places. It's amateur, but beautiful and striking in its own way. What's more striking than the border is the verse written in a swirling script.

"Love is patient, love is kind, it does not envy, it does not boast. It is not proud. It is not rude. It is not self-seeking, it is not easily angered. It keeps no record of wrongs."

I flip the card open to find a cursive message. It's the kind of cursive that's hard to read, all loops and scrolls, but also its own form of art. It takes me a minute, but I muddle out the words—even the ones that are misspelled.

Dearest June,

On your wedding day, I wish to give you one piece of advice. Times are changing, and you will change too, but I pray you never forget your roots. We will never forget you. No matter where the wind blows you, you will always be our daughter.

The only thing you need to know about marriage is in the Bible—1 Corinthians 13.

Love forgives.

God bless you on your marriage, June.

It's not signed, but it must be from Meemaw's own mother. A woman I know next to nothing about except that she lived a hard life of poverty.

Tears drip steadily down my cheeks as I consider the words on the card. A Bible verse. Somehow, this card feels more precious than anything made of gold, or silver, or rubies.

Love forgives.

Those words etch themselves deeply on my heart, carving into the stone there. But even before that wisdom, the phrase *love is patient…*

They're the same words Paige said to me.

The same words Meemaw said to me.

The same words Mom said to me before I came to West Virginia when I was bemoaning my terrible luck with men.

I stare at the card a little harder because these words are significant. I feel them settling over me like a blanket of warmth. I want to take in every detail, every thought that's bouncing around my mind, as I look at the words and try to make sense of them. I don't know how, in one single verse, so much is contained, but it's clear the entire world, and then some, is there.

Something plinks against my window, and I look up.

Another plink, and it can't be a coincidence. I swipe the tears away and gently place the card on my bed before walking to the window and brushing aside the sheer curtains.

Beck stands below with a handful of pebbles as he tosses them softly against the glass. His serious face is drawn, his eyes searching the window, and I know the moment he sees me because he relaxes his shoulders before tensing up again.

Love forgives.

I open the window.

"Yes?" I whisper, even though it's the middle of the day and we're two adults, but something about this has me feeling like it calls for clandestine behavior.

"Brooke, I…" Beck drops the rocks and steps closer. Because Meemaw's house is built into a hillside, my window is only a half story above the ground. His head is visible over the sill, but the rest of his body disappears as he comes up to the screen. "I'm so sorry."

I sniff, and for a moment, I think about playing high and mighty and making him figure it out. But that's not me either. I've always been a direct communicator, and he should know that. If he thinks he loves me, he needs to know that.

"You chose her. Over me. After you said you loved me."

"I know. And I don't have good boundaries with people, and that wasn't right. She was calling from Ben's phone, but I shouldn't have answered anyone right then." He swallows hard, and his neck cords. "I don't want her, Brooke," he says before lowering his voice to something quieter than a whisper. "I want you."

I nod my head yes and blow out a breath because *love forgives*, and as I look into his sincere brown eyes, there is no doubt in my mind that I do love the man before me.

He's imperfect, but so am I.

The moment calls for one thing. I pop the screen out and push it aside, just like I would in case of a fire. Then I climb up on the window sill and hop down into Dr. Beckett Whistler's waiting arms.

MEEMAW

June is beginning to think that this situation with Dr. Beckett and her granddaughter is taking too long. In her mind, they should have been married last week. Three dates is more than enough time for two very smart people to realize they need one another. She wheels her knee scooter down the hallway to Brooke's bedroom and knocks once.

No answer.

She knocks again, louder this time.

Still no answer.

June pushes the door open and is greeted by several things. First, the card her mother gave her on her wedding day sitting on the bed. Second, the sheer curtains fluttering in the breeze and the window screen popped out. Third, and most interesting, is that her granddaughter and her neighbor's heads are visible through the very open window, and they are most certainly kissing.

June watches for a brief moment before collecting herself and slowly wheeling backward out of the room and back to her couch.

She has news to tell her friends and a church to book for a wedding, but her phone is not where she left it.

She shrugs and then bends to retrieve the old laptop that lives on the bottom shelf of the coffee table. Blowing dust off the case, she opens it up and logs onto Facebook. In her excitement, she types out an update.

> Help! I need to book a church for a wedding, and fast! Finally, one of my grandbabies is getting married!

The likes fly in, the comments roll in like a tide, and June is happy as she basks in the online attention.

Outside, the young couple continues kissing and whispering promises to one another, while inside both of their respective dwellings, their phones buzz.

Again, and again, and again.

31

BROOKE

I waltz into my room after what can only be described as the best kisses of my life.

Sighing contentedly, I flop on my bed and smile. Meemaw was on her computer when I walked in, and I feel a little like I have a delicious surprise to give her when she's done with whatever it is she's focused on.

Beck wants me. My grandmother's gruff, brusque neighbor who hides his heart of gold and caring nature behind a stony exterior because of his past wants *me*. And not just in the way other men have wanted me. He wants a *future* with me.

I can't help it, I kick my feet and let out a quiet squeal because of all the things that have happened today, this is the most unexpected. I know Paige and Connor are celebrating their good news, but I really need to tell her. She was right. Being patient was worth it. Now I get to say that Dr. Beckett Whistler is my boyfriend. Not just the guy I like and think likes me back, but actually a real *boyfriend*.

Bubbles fizz through my body like a carbonated drink as I look around the room for my phone. There it is, lying face-down across the room from where I threw it earlier.

With a spring in my step, I bound off the bed to tell Paige the good news. I'm not so bad of a friend that I'll call her, but I will text her 'You were right about being patient' and a kissy face emoji. She'll call and talk this through with me when she gets a chance.

When I flip my phone over to start composing the text, I stop and drop it back to the floor.

I have 397 texts.

I have 48 missed calls, all from my mother.

Someone died.

Without hesitation, and with my heart in my throat, I call my mom. She answers on the first ring.

"Brooke!" Mom yells into the phone.

"Mom? What's wrong?" I stutter.

"How could you NOT tell me?"

"How could I not tell you what?" I ask, scratching my head, because it doesn't sound like someone died.

"That you're getting married! How could you do this to me! You can't just go off and get married in West Virginia to any old guy you meet! And another thing, young lady, he never asked your father for his permission, and I don't know what's gotten into you. OH NO. Brooke, are you in trouble?" She pauses for a breath, but my jaw is on the floor, and I can't quite formulate a response to everything she just said.

She thinks I'm getting married?

She thinks I'm in trouble?

"You truly thought that letting me find out through Mom's Facebook was going to be enough communication? Where is the wedding? Is it IN West Virginia? Wouldn't you have it up here at our church?"

I shake my head to try to clear the barrage of questions away. If I'm nicknamed 'the general,' she should be nicknamed 'the artillery,' because this is a rapid-fire assault.

One phrase she says lands deep in my chest.

"Mom?" I say, fighting down the urge to scream and keeping my voice as collected as I can. She stops speaking for a moment. "What do you mean you found out through your mom's Facebook?"

"My mom posted an update about an hour ago, where she said she needed to book a church for a wedding because one of her grandbabies was finally getting married."

My eyes widen. "Meemaw said that?"

"Yes."

"On the internet?"

"Yes."

My happiness shrivels up faster than a grape turns into a raisin in the West Virginia sun.

"I don't understand … she doesn't know yet…"

"BROOKE BELLE BASTION, YOU TELL ME RIGHT NOW WHAT SHE DOESN'T KNOW."

I pull the phone away from my ear at the absurd decibel she's managed to achieve.

"I … I don't know why she said that. On the internet. I hadn't even told her that I have a boyfriend."

"Boyfriend?" Mom questions, at a more reasonable decibel.

"Yeah. I just. It just happened. Like an hour ago … oh no. She saw us kiss … and she assumed … and now…"

"My mom put the cart way before the horse?"

"Yes. But it's on the internet," I say as I crumple into a heap on the pink shag carpet. "And Beck has his own story, and…" I dissolve into sobs.

"Honey," Mom says, her voice significantly softer now. "You can tell her to take it down."

"But it's still out *there*, Mom," I whine. "I have hundreds of texts, and now I have to tell everyone what she did."

"Sweetheart… It's quite likely that she's not totally right in her mind."

I roll my eyes. Meemaw is definitely in her right mind, except for this post. It's so strange. She's been known to make questionable decisions a time or two, and definitely to not think through the full implications of her actions. But this is the first time I'm wondering if she really is starting to slip.

The thought squeezes my conscience. Whether she was fully aware of what she was implying when she posted that, it needs to come down.

I pull as much courage as I can muster and walk out the door of my room to face Meemaw and have a stern conversation with her about boundaries.

As I walk, I skim through my texts. There are at least ninety from Matt asking me *what?* And other friends texting me ring emojis and congratulations memes. Paige's text says, "We need to talk."

I start to text her back, but stop when I hear Beck's voice in Meemaw's living room.

"Take. It. Down. June," he says through gritted teeth. "You had no right to do that to me or Brooke."

I peek to the side to see Meemaw sitting tight-lipped on the sofa, her head hanging low. Beck pulls out his phone. "Miss Lily, Miss Rose, Miss Sharon, Miss Ruth, *and* Miss Helena all called to ask me why I haven't brought my new girl around! June! I haven't had a *new* girl for more than twenty minutes, and now the entire community thinks we're getting married! Did you think about that?"

"I'm sorry," Meemaw says to the ground, and a tear slips down her cheeks. "I just really want to see my Brooke happy."

Beck softens. He walks to Meemaw's spot on the couch and drops onto the cushion next to her. He turns slightly and catches me, his eyes full of some unidentifiable emotion. "Miss June," he says slowly and then draws in a breath as he locks his gaze with me. "I want Brooke to be happy too. I want nothing more than that. But that's *our* business to decide."

Meemaw shakes her head in agreement. "I…" she stutters. "I know that, but I just plain old got excited and forgot that I shouldn't do that."

Beck meets her eyes with all seriousness and whispers. "June, are you forgetting things more often these days?"

Meemaw nods.

"Have you mentioned that to your doctor?"

Meemaw shakes her head.

Beck scrubs a hand down his face and frowns. "Can I help you make an appointment with the specialist? I'll take you if it's on my day off."

Meemaw bobs her head, but it's like a light has gone out and all of her youthful virility has vanished.

32

BECK

I hadn't really suspected things were going on with June's memory, but maybe I should have. She's just always been so eccentric that it's hard to know what's a problem and what's simply June being June.

Brooke hovers in the hallway, her fist over her mouth as she watches me ask June about her memory and seeing a specialist. When she agrees to go see a specialist, Brooke lets out a sob and flees down the hall.

I glance at June, who shakes her head sadly with a wry smile. "You should go…" Her voice cracks. "You should go to her." She pats my hand with her own leathery one and tips her head toward the hallway.

I squeeze her hand back before I stand and then stride down the hallway. Brooke's door is ajar, and she's flopped on the twin bed, sobs wracking her body. I knock lightly once, but Brooke must not hear because she doesn't so much as look at the door. I push it open a little more and knock louder.

This time, her red-rimmed eyes and splotchy cheeks rise to meet mine. She wipes her eyes furiously, but it doesn't make a difference.

"Sorry." She hiccups.

"Can I come in?" I ask, keeping my voice as soothing as possible.

When she nods, I cross the threshold, and propriety be darned, I go straight to Brooke on the bed. She scoots over and draws her knees to her chest, where she wraps her arms around them.

She sniffles, and I can't take it. I sit down next to her and wrap my arms around her. She leans into me, and the wetness on my shirt tells me she's crying again.

"Brooke," I whisper against her blonde and pink hair that smells like lavender. "Brooke, it's ok. There are medications we can try... There are things that we can do to help..."

Brooke looks up sharply, and reflected in the depths of her eyes is a pain unlike any I've ever seen before. "Mom said that no one knew if she was becoming more eccentric in her old age or losing her faculties."

I give a small chuckle. "It's hard to tell with June."

"I don't want to lose her, Beck."

"Honey." The endearment rolls off my tongue. "Honey, you're not losing her. We're helping her."

"Beck?" she stutters as she extracts herself from my hug and begins toying with the fringed edge of the comforter. "If you ... knew something ... would you do something crazy?"

Confusion washes over me. "What do you mean, sweetheart?"

Another endearment? Who am I? Oh wait, I'm the man in love.

"Uh... It's just that it's the one thing she ... really wants," Brooke mumbles to the floor.

I can't figure it out.

"I'm going to need you to spell it out for me. I have no idea what you mean."

Brooke's eyes shift to mine for a half beat before she looks away and murmurs, "Never mind," to the carpet.

At that moment, it all clicks into place. Brooke is asking me if I'd marry her before June's memory gets worse.

While I will absolutely do that, I'm not willing to rush to the courthouse right now. I didn't rush with Addie, but I ignored warning signs for years. One of them was Addie's refusal to get married at my church. She didn't have a faith; she just wanted a pretty venue.

Truthfully, June is in the early stages of whatever *this* is, and Brooke is reeling from this information coming to light.

I pull Brooke next to me, and I rest my chin against her shoulder as I clasp my hands around her. "Brooke, I promise I will ask you to marry me if it's right. But today is not the day, and June has more time than you think."

Brooke turns and meets my eyes with her soulful ones. "Really?" She bites her lip, and I inhale to keep myself from kissing all this tension away.

"Really," I say.

Brooke leans into me, planting her lips on mine and kisses me deeply. My fingers tangle in her hair, and I'm just about to shift her to a more comfortable position when a very loud "AHEM" sounds from the hall.

"I said to get her, not *ahem* with her," June calls.

We were *not* doing that, but if June hadn't interrupted, I don't know what would have happened, so I'm glad she did.

"Young lady, I know I said if hanky-panky happened, I'd get you two married, but I don't think you understood. It's not supposed to happen in my house."

Brooke giggles as she stands up. There's no shame in her countenance. "Sorry, Meemaw." She sniffs. "I just really like him."

"Well, hopefully he puts several rings on it soon. An engagement ring *and* a wedding band, and then you can hanky-panky as much as you'd like."

And just like that, June's back.

I scrub a hand down my face, letting the calluses on my fingers catch on the stubble of my five o'clock shadow. I blow out a breath before I stand, and when I do, I link my fingers with Brooke's.

"Miss June." I meet her eyes with my own direct gaze. "I promise you I'll take care of Brooke. But you have to let us do this on our own timeline." I swallow as I turn my face to meet Brooke's eyes momentarily and then back to June's. "No matter what happens, June. I'm not going to rush this. It means too much to me."

June's brow furrows, but she gives one succinct nod from where she stands with her knee on the scooter.

I sense it's time to leave, so I bring Brooke's knuckles to my lips and plant a kiss there before I let go. As I pass by June, she reaches out, slightly off-kilter. Her palm lands on my forearm, and my hands steady her slight frame.

"Thank you, young man," she whispers.

I'm sure she's not talking about going to the specialist with me.

33

BROOKE

Beck left, and now it's just me and Meemaw.

"Why didn't you tell me?" I whisper.

"Brookie…" she trails off. "It's not that bad. I just sometimes forget that doing things the way I decide to do them is unsafe."

"But why didn't you tell Mom? You *knew*," I accuse.

Meemaw sighs. Her lips curve into a deep frown, and the wrinkles on her face look as deep as the New River Gorge. My heart cracks. "I don't think I really know anything until I see the specialist your doctor Beck wants me to see."

"Fine," I huff. "But why did you ignore it?"

"Because is it just me living my life and being eccentric, or is there something wrong with my brain?" She taps her forehead with her knuckles. "Some questions you just plumb don't want answered."

I accept her answer as a fair one, even if I'm still hurt and worried. I'm the human equivalent of a tangled yarn ball of emotions.

"Brookie…" Meemaw sighs. "I just want to see you happy."

"Meemaw." My eyes brim with tears as I cross the room to give her a hug. "I know you do."

She squeezes me as best she can from her awkward position on the scooter. She sniffles in a breath and then, in a shaky voice, says, "I can't find my phone."

I pull back a little. "Is that why you were using the laptop?"
She nods.

"Then let's go find it."

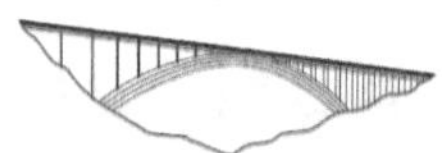

I didn't find Meemaw's phone until early this morning before work. One of my socks had a little pebble or *something* irritating in the toe seam, so I plopped on the couch to fix it. Inadvertently, I sat on the crack between cushions. With a huff, the worn couch spread apart, and I found myself sitting on Meemaw's phone.

I had been nervous about leaving her without a phone while I went to work. Her specialist appointment is in two days, and despite Beck saying he'd take her, I know that's why I'm here. I'm here to take Meemaw to doctor appointments, to be good company, and to help her with things around the house.

So far, Meemaw's fiercely clung to her independence, and my job has been to keep a bemused eye on her. The weight of what we're dealing with hangs heavy on my heart, but she insisted I go to work.

"How will you ever make friends if you're stuck inside with an old lady all day?"

It was a valid question, and she assured me she was just fine, so off I went to work.

I pull out of the driveway and turn the behemoth vehicle through the mountain roads. When I arrive at work, I'm more than a little exhausted from holding all the fragments of my heart together by sheer will.

"Hey, Brooke!" Logan calls from a perch atop a stack of gear. He appears to be tying a rope knot around supplies for the big day trip he's leading, but he stands in the direct light of the sun, and I can't make it out entirely.

I throw my hand over my forehead to shield my eyes just as he hops down from the top.

Logan takes one look at me before he murmurs, "Whoa. What happened?"

Inexplicably, I, the woman known as 'the general' because I am always in control, lose the grip on my firmly tethered emotions. The feelings take off, and despite the fact that I'm standing in front of a man I hardly know, I start to cry. And not just cry—*ugly* cry.

Logan opens his arms, and I step into them for a hug. It's strange, but I know that Logan, the serial dater of tourists, isn't hitting on me. He's doing nothing more than offering comfort to a friend.

I pull back after a minute and swipe my hands across my wet lashes. My hand comes away covered with mascara.

I blow out a breath and whisper, "Sorry."

He gives the half smile that probably makes all the tourist women want to date him in the first place, but it has no effect on me. "You want to take a minute? We've got an hour before the group should start showing up, but I can handle anyone who's early."

"Thanks." I meet his blue eyes as I walk behind the counter. I grab a key to the storage shed as I pass by since it's one place where I can have a little privacy to compose myself. The last thing I hear as I slip through the door is Logan's voice saying the words *your girl*.

Finally alone, I slump to the ground, pull my knees to my chest, and hug them tight. I sit like that for a while, putting my hand just under the collar of my shirt so I'm touching my collarbone, and focus on breathing. I had not anticipated that living with Meemaw would be so difficult for my emotional regulation. When I had my own apartment and was upset, I had a place I felt safe to let it all out. With

Meemaw, I haven't been able to do that because I've internalized my role as caretaker. Just because I am helping her doesn't mean I don't have feelings too.

I'm sure my face is a fright, but I have a job to do, so now that I've let some of the emotional explosion out, I'm ready to face the task at hand. Maybe not as cheerfully as I would usually, but I can grit my teeth and get through this shift with some semblance of normalcy.

The grit stuck to my jean shorts plinks to the ground as I stand, so I sweep my backside with my hand before I pull on the door handle. I don't get to the door because, as I'm still brushing the floor off my shorts, the door swings open.

A man stands in the middle of the doorway, squinting into the darkness of the storage shed.

"Brooke?" Beck's voice is hoarse. "Are you in here?"

I step forward from the corner where I'd been slumped against the wall, and in the backlight of the sunshine, I can see his face. His arched eyebrows, his lips turned down at the corners, the worry in his brown eyes, the backward hat on his head. I have the advantage because my eyes have already adjusted to the light before his do to the dark.

As soon as he sees me, he steps forward with long, confident strides. "Brooke." He reaches out a thumb and brushes some lingering wetness off my cheek. "Why are you crying?"

"Me–" I sniffle. "Meemaw."

Beck opens his arms, and I step into them with no hesitation. Unlike the hug with Logan earlier, this hug has meaning I can't deny. His gray T-shirt is soft against my cheek, and I let myself listen to the steady thump of his heartbeat. His hand rubs patterns over the back of my pink New RAFT T-shirt as he holds me.

My own arms wrap around his waist and squeeze as tight as I can, knowing that he's holding me. He's with me.

Finally, I release my arms and step back. "How did you know I was crying in here?"

Beck rubs a hand down the side of his face. "Logan told me."

"Oh." I had hoped he was just coming to see me. Disappointment must flash across my face because Beck takes one step closer.

"I did want to come see you at work, though. I just didn't want to distract you when you're still getting the hang of it."

I smile at the sincerity in his tone. "Thanks for coming to see me anyway," I say as I slip my hand in his.

He pulls the door away from the rock wedge with his other hand, and we step out into the sunshine together. To the left, Logan's clicking away on the computer as he talks on the phone, but there's a strange woman staring at the door to the storage shed.

"Beckett," she says sternly, her mouth turned into a frown that looks oddly familiar and her brown eyes snapping as she glances my way. "Is it true?"

Beck drops my hand as if he's been scalded. I look from one to the other at least twice before Beckett provides the answer to the riddle.

"Mom."

34

BECK

My mother is standing in front of me, but she's *not* staring at me. She's staring at Brooke. Natasha Whistler is an intimidating woman on the best of days. It is clear that today is not the best of days because the look on her face is far worse than intimidating. She is a formidable fortress. Her iron-gray hair is the castle keep, and she is ready to pour boiling tar on her opponents.

Unfortunately, the way I dropped Brooke's hand makes everything about this interaction ten times worse. I can't decide if I should pick it back up, or if I should step forward and give my mom a hug to break the tension. And because I am a highly educated man with a medical degree, I do neither.

"Who is *this?*" my mom hisses, her brown eyes locked on Brooke's petite frame, and a snarl curling her lips.

I swallow. This is bad. My mom has always been protective of the ones she loves. It's just unfortunate she loved Addie more than me. My mother has pestered me to get back together with Addie at least once a month since Addie walked out on our wedding. I only speak to my mother once a month because I cannot stand the tension she brings to every interaction.

Brooke breaks the tension with a bright smile as she steps forward. "Hi," she says, extending her hand to my mom. "I'm Brooke Bastion. Beck's neighbor for the summer."

My mother's lip slowly unfurls from a snarl into a determined smile of dislike. It's rather like the Grinch when he steals all the Who's presents.

"Ah. For the *summer*." She cuts her eyes to me, and I catch her meaning, but she does stretch out her hand and shake Brooke's.

"Brooke is my girlfriend," I blurt out, unnerved by what my mom is implying. Brooke isn't just some summer fling. She's certainly not a casual hookup, and she's definitely not temporary. Is it too soon to think about marriage? Yes, but I already am. That's what you do when you *love* someone.

"Sure," Mom says with a knowing glint in her eyes that says she does not believe me at all.

"No, really, Mom." I step closer to Brooke and wrap my arm around her. "Brooke and I are together."

"Beckett, I understand. You're a man. You have needs. You don't have to pretend that this hussy is something she clearly isn't just because you're sleeping with her."

I cannot hear because of the roaring in my ears. I cannot breathe for the thousand-pound animal that has decided to sit on my chest. And I cannot stand still as the blood in my veins goes from calm to a rapid boil.

"How dare you," I grind through clenched teeth. My hands curl into fists at my sides, and it's all I can do to keep myself from shaking my mom until she stops being awful. There's not much of a chance of that happening, so I shove my hands in my pockets instead.

"Honey," Mom condescends to Brooke. "He's had a good thing before, and—" She gives Brooke a scathing look from her feet to her hair. "Quite frankly, dear, you have *pink* hair, and you are not what he needs. He's a successful doctor, and you're … what, a tour guide for the summer? Really, Beckett." She clucks her tongue, and my muscles snap and pop as I hold myself back from erupting.

I grunt. Cavemen have decided to inhabit my body momentarily because any form of language has left me. All that's possible for me now is rage. The kind that vibrates through your body and has supersonic effects on those around you. Everyone around me but my mother.

"Leave," I say in my most commanding voice. It's one I rarely use outside of work, and never with my mother.

I don't know if it's enough to tell my mother to go, so I turn only to see that Brooke's fury matches my own. Her own body shakes, yet she has a neutral face, and when she speaks, her voice is deathly calm.

"Mrs. Whistler," Brooke says in an even tone, stepping closer to my mom and invading her personal space. "You don't scare me."

And then, in a twist I don't see coming at all, Brooke turns around and launches herself into my arms for a very performative kiss. Her lips crash into mine, and it's clear that this is a battle that she is going to win. She is determined to not stop kissing me until her point has been made. I'm not sure *how* her kissing me is proving her point and not supporting my mom's earlier implications, except for the fact that she is showing she isn't scared of my mom's catty tactics.

After several minutes, Brooke breaks away to catch her breath. I wrap my arm around her waist and pull her close to me.

"Mom." I give her a single head bob. "Don't insult Brooke again."

"Oh, please." Mom's frustration mounts as she stiffens, and her tone becomes even more condescending. "You really want to waste your breath on this?" She points one finger at Brooke.

"I'd waste everything on her and still be a rich man," I retort.

Mom's eyebrows raise a fraction of an inch. "I know it's not serious because you would have told me if it were."

"I know it's serious *because* I didn't tell you. You have no business interfering in my life now. You made it clear you sided with Addie, and I have no interest in seeing you or Addie again. Goodbye, Mom."

"And the wedding?" Mom asks, because she doesn't get the hint that she's not welcome here and that this conversation is over.

"You're not invited," I snap at the exact same time Brooke says, "There is no wedding."

"No wedding?" Mom asks, a hint of confusion cracking her stone façade.

"Not yet," I huff, squeezing Brooke tighter to me. "But soon."

To make my point, I place a kiss on the crown of Brooke's head.

"But Addie said that it was on Facebook. I knew I had to come and see for myself."

"Yes, because Addie and Facebook are the most reliable sources of information."

"Don't be smart with me, young man. I stopped at your house first, but when you weren't there, I asked your neighbor. The old woman at the house with the green door. She said she thought you'd be here."

"Meemaw…" Brooke whispers a sigh and starts to run a hand through her hair.

"Mom," I say slowly, deliberately. "You need to go. I mean it."

"But Beckett, I'm your mother." There's a slight hitch in her voice, the tiniest bit of sorrow in her words, but I can't buy it. Her stone façade might be cracking, but my body is made of granite. I am an impenetrable fortress, and although I realized long ago what my mother is, I'm no longer willing to make exceptions for her because she birthed me.

"And I'm not willing to let you insult the woman I love."

Mom's eyes flash something that might be regret, but I turn away, grasp Brooke's hand, and tug her away from my second least favorite woman in the world.

I don't let go, and I don't stop walking until we're on the other side of the storage shed and sheltered from prying eyes.

35

BROOKE

I am not scared of petty women. I'm not afraid of women who are overgrown mean girls. I'm not frightened by bullies. I never have been. But there is no doubt in my mind that Beck's mom is petty, an overgrown mean girl, and a bully, all in one. Sure, I'm angry because she made it very clear that all I am in her eyes is a passing floozy. Mostly, though, I'm angry at how she treated Beck, and weirdly, I'm not angry at all.

Words are hard for him. And instead of clamming up completely like I half expected him to, he defended me. If there's anything more attractive than a man standing up for a woman, I'd like to know about it because nothing else comes to mind.

Beck breathes heavily once we're behind the shed and locks eyes with me. An entire world of emotion swirls through his gaze, and I'm debating kissing him again (because I want to, not because I have a point to make), when Logan's voice floats out of the shadows.

"Your mom is still … like that?"

Beck's head snaps around until he finds Logan lurking in the corners. "Yep," he says, and there's a lifetime of frustration in the single syllable.

Logan purses his lips and shakes his head. "Addie?"

"Yep," Beck says again.

Logan steps forward into the light. "I'm sorry, man." He claps a hand on Beck's shoulder. "Don't let them ruin your life." He looks slyly at me and winks. "And Beck, I *will* be needing my employee up front in ten minutes."

Beck gives one slow nod as Logan walks away, but he doesn't break eye contact with me. It's intense, and I don't know if I should run for the hills or stay exactly where I am and see what this attractive man who cares enough about me to declare his love to his terrible mother is thinking. I'm unsteady, and that's rare for me. Rare, and somewhat thrilling.

I take a half step backward, and my back bumps into the wall of the storage building.

Beck takes a half step forward, and I lean toward him in response. His arms land on either side of my shoulders, his hands braced against the back wall. "Brooke," he whispers. "I am so sorry."

And then he takes control and leans in for a sweet kiss. It's not hurried or passionate. It's soft and gentle, and it makes me want a lifetime with this man. He breaks the kiss and presses his lips right on the scar at the corner of my eye. When he's done, he pulls away, and his liquid brown eyes meet mine.

"So that's your mom?" I ask, because I'm undone, and I don't know how to break the tension of what's building between us. I don't want to break it. I want to stand on the precipice and jump with Beck and trust that no matter where we fall, we'll land together.

"Y-yeah," Beck stammers as he drops his hands to his sides. "She's not very nice, but I haven't ever cut ties completely because she paid for so much of my education. And she's my…" He squeezes his eyes shut.

"She's your mom," I say.

He opens his eyes, and I see the sorrow in them, the hurt that this woman has inflicted on her own child, and the love that Beck still has for the woman who birthed him despite everything I just saw.

"Yeah," he says roughly. He steps back, out of my space, and I find myself unappreciative of the new distance between us.

Thoughts swirl in my mind like water circling a drain, but one has to be asked. "What does Addie have to do with your mom?"

Beck kicks a pebble with his shoe. "My mom really appreciated Addie's…" He frowns. "Genetics."

"What?" That answer is strange.

"She liked the thought of grandchildren … looking a certain way."

"Oh." I'm a balloon, and those words just depleted me of all helium. The self-doubt that I shoved aside claws its way back out of the place I thought I'd buried it. Addie is beautiful, model-esque, and I'm not. I've always had a 'girl next door' type of beauty, not the 'sells makeup in magazines' type.

"No, Brooke." Beck's eyes widen and he shakes his head. "Addie is *not* more beautiful than you." Somehow, he sees it. He sees the anxiety I hide, and more than that, in just a few dates, he *knows* me.

The sincerity in his eyes makes me almost believe him. But there are still objective truths.

"Yeah, but I have pink hair," I whisper.

Beck leans down toward my ear. "I don't think that's genetic."

In spite of everything—the heaviness of what I've been dealing with regarding Meemaw's declining health, the fact that Beck's mother just appeared and attempted to bully me and him out of a relationship, and that Beck found me crying in a storage shed before work, *and* that I am at work—laughter bubbles up.

Beck smiles and pulls me in for a hug. He leans his cheek against my head, and I allow myself to rest in the certainty that this man is unlike any other I've met. This man is the one. It's a strange fact of the heart, but just like you can't see the air you breathe, you *know* it's there. I can't see the love I'm feeling, but I *know* it's real.

Maybe it's a primal instinct, maybe it's years of awful casual dates that I had hoped would turn into a serious relationship, but now that I'm wrapped in the strong arms of a man who loves me without a shadow of a doubt, there's nothing else for me to say except to whisper the words he hasn't heard from me yet.

"I love you too."

36

BECK

I am used to women demanding things from me. Brooke *doesn't*. I was used to Addie talking about how much she loved the status of me being a doctor. Brooke doesn't seem to care that my job has a level of prestige. Over time, I tuned out Addie's determination to look down on people. I'm embarrassed that I overlooked so much because of her physical beauty. And yet, Brooke's beautiful too. I see in subtle cues that she doesn't think she's equal to Addie. I can also see that Brooke has a confidence that allows her to brush self-doubts aside. The fact that she struggles a little with comparing herself to Addie shows me that she *cares*. And the fact that she laughed at my joke about pink hair shows me that she will face struggles and trials with humor. Laughing about things is something that Addie and I did at first, but as time went on, laughter became more and more sparse, until we never laughed about anything.

When Brooke whispered "I love you too" to me, I was ready to drop to my knees and propose to her.

I did not, because I am not insane, and I understand that we need more time to date. But after years of suffocating my feelings under a blanket of work, now that they are breathing again, the feelings are determined to make the most of every situation. It's YOLO, *carpe diem*, and *veni, vidi, vici* all at once.

Brooke went to go do her actual job, and I climbed into my car to drive back home. There is an important conversation with June that I need to have.

I park my truck in the driveway. Addie's needling me about buying a vehicle more befitting a doctor prickles under my skin because, for the first time in the better part of a decade, I find myself honestly considering buying a new truck. Not because Brooke has ever said anything, but because she hasn't even batted an eye at this old vehicle, and I am in need of an upgrade.

When I knock on June's door, she answers immediately. Her surgery recovery is going well, and she can move with just a walking boot now.

"Beckett," she says with a toothy grin.

"Miss June," I reply, swiping my ball cap off my head and holding it in my hands. "May I come in?"

"I never say no to a neighborly visit." The glint in her eye makes me think she knows what I'm up to, but there's no way she does. "Come on in and sit yourself down."

I toe off my shoes before I cross to the faded floral couch. June's walking boot thumps as she returns from the kitchen with a glass of lemonade.

"Brooke made it," she says as she sets a blue glass on a coaster.

I smile in appreciation and because the mention of Brooke makes me smile. For so long, the very name of women elicited a frown, but now I'm smiling. *Who even am I?*

"Thank you." I take a sip. "Miss June…" Nerves tighten my throat.

"Yes?"

"I want to ask Brooke to marry me."

"Isn't it a little soon for that?"

"Yes, probably too soon," I say. "But I can't deny it." I scratch my chin. "Do you happen to know what Brooke's ring size is?"

June cackles. "No one knows their ring size off the top of their head, but I suspect I can help you out."

"Addie did," I mumble, the memories of the last time I went ring shopping fighting their way back into my consciousness. To be fair, Addie also knew all the 'c's' that go with ring shopping and had specific expectations about what I could purchase for her. She was most concerned with the 'c' for carat, and nothing less than two would do. It was agonizing to know I was expected to get it just right, surprise her, and somehow still meet her high demands and expectations.

I shake my head and reach out to pat June's hand. "About Brooke, I … I want to talk to her family. And I was hoping you'd share their contact information with me."

She smiles. "I think that's a lovely idea, young man."

I have to give June credit, this is by far the most normal interaction I've ever had with her.

She extends a hand, and I reach mine out to shake hers, but she pulls her hand away.

"No, silly boy," June says. "Here." She stands and thumps down the hallway. I wait for her, but she calls, "Come, Beckett."

I follow her into her room. The gauzy curtains let in light, the neatly made bed in the middle of the room has an old and faded wedding ring patterned quilt, and there are piles of books and notecards spread throughout the room. Sticky notes are on the walls with messages. I know enough to know that these are a sign of some cognitive decline, and it breaks my heart.

"Here you go, young man." June turns from the dresser and extends her hand to me. There, set on her wrinkled, leathery hand, is a gold band with a single teardrop-shaped ruby. June shakes a little as she gazes down at the jewelry, and I can see how special this ring is to her.

"Miss June," I say, reaching out and picking the ring off her palm. "It's beautiful."

More words aren't needed for June to open up about this, and when she tells me the story, I'm glad she did.

"Does Brooke know this story?" I ask.

"No," June replies. "I've been saving the ring and the story for her, but now…" She breaks off and looks at the window for a moment before turning her attention back to me. "Now I'm not sure I'll be able to remember it when the time comes."

If my heart was broken before, it's shattered now. June MacCord is many things to me. Mostly, she's been an annoying neighbor, but I see her in a different light. I see her as the older, eccentric woman who is determined to live her life to the fullest as she senses her abilities changing. A woman who loves fiercely and has wisdom that I can only dream of, because it's not the sort of thing you learn from books. No, June's wisdom is the sort of thing you learn from a hard life and trust in God's grace.

"Miss June," I whisper, meeting her gaze. "Thank you. I will keep the story and tell it to her when it's time." A post-it note flutters in the breeze, and an idea takes hold. "Do you think you might like to write the story down? I could hold on to it and give it to her with the ring when the time is right."

June smiles broadly. "That is an excellent idea."

I swallow against the emotion clogging my throat. "Did you make an appointment? With the specialist I recommended?"

June's eyes close. "It's tomorrow."

"Do you want me to take you?"

June's eyes shine with emotion. She nods. "I think it will be hard for Brooke if the…" She swallows. "If the news isn't good."

I bob my head, and June's blue eyes shine with tears. It won't be hard for just Brooke. June will need someone with her too. I open my arms to her, and she steps into them for a grandmotherly hug.

I don't know when I started seeing June MacCord as more than my nosy old neighbor, but I know I'll be with her through this.

MEEMAW

June MacCord knows her memory isn't what it once was. She also knows that her neighbor and her granddaughter are destined for each other. When Beckett's mother appeared on June's doorstep, she knew how serious things were. Women like Natasha Whistler are infamous even among the older generation.

Yes, June overstepped with her social media posts, but that's been taken down, and a message posted that apologized for the confusion. Now June sits at the table, waiting for her neighbor to drive her and her granddaughter to the specialist. A card is tucked into an envelope bearing the name "the future Mrs. Brooke Whistler," and that envelope is tucked in her bag.

Brooke is blow-drying her hair in the bathroom, and the soft hum of noise is loud enough that when Beck knocks on the door, Brooke won't hear him.

June drums her fingers along the oak table while she waits.

A soft knock at the door, and June springs into action. She opens the door and smiles into the warm brown eyes of the man who will soon be her grandson. "Beckett."

"Miss June," he says, sweeping his worn gray baseball cap off his head and walking through the threshold.

"I have this for you," she whispers conspiratorially as she extends the envelope to him.

He takes it with slightly shaky hands, and June has a glimpse of nerves that make her giddy. This man is perfect for her granddaughter because while the man himself is not perfect, the man *cares*.

Loud music sounds from the road as a delivery truck drives by. Obnoxious beeps startle the older woman and the younger man from their moment as their heads turn toward the road.

"Did you order something?" the younger man asks.

June shrugs.

The truck continues backing up the steep driveway until it's close to the walkway. A man in a brown delivery uniform hops out and strolls across the path with a clipboard in hand.

"June MacCord?" he inquires.

"Yes?" June replies.

"Great. It will be a while—one hundred and eighteen cast-iron skillets are really hard to unload."

37

BROOKE

When I walk out of the bathroom, freshly showered and ready to face this appointment with Meemaw, I am met by the unexpected on several counts.

First, Beck stands next to Meemaw by the front door, his mouth agape. Second, a delivery man holds a clipboard with a receipt that has been folded and looped over multiple times before being secured under the clip. The delivery man continues unlooping it until the receipt is a trail of paper that blows in the wind like a kite string. It trails down the porch steps and onto the walkway.

"One hundred and eighteen cast-iron pans. You'll just need to sign here," he says.

Beck's jaw snaps shut. His muscled forearms are tense, and the muscles pop when he crosses them over his chest. "Don't sign that." He looks from the delivery man to the receipt. "Clearly, there's been a mistake."

The delivery man checks the address and sizes up Meemaw. "You June MacCord?"

"Yes…" Meemaw's voice wavers.

"You know you ordered one hundred and eighteen cast-iron skillets?"

"Do I look crazy to you?" Meemaw says, turning her Southern lady charm on. I know West Virginia isn't exactly Southern in the truest sense of the word, but the woman knows how to challenge the menfolk.

"Blimey. This is a mess." Delivery Man shakes his head. "No, ma'am, you do not look crazy."

"Good," Beck cuts in. "Because, June, how many skillets did you intend to order?"

"Four. Who needs one hundred and eighteen?"

"Why would you order four?" Beck asks, the muscles along his jaw ticking as his jaw clenches.

"One for each burner," Meemaw responds as if it's the most basic of facts.

The delivery man nods as if that makes perfect sense.

"But, Meemaw," I say, breaking into the conversation and startling everyone. "The burners are all different sizes. And you already have cast-iron skillets."

"Hmmm." Delivery Man purses his lips and wipes his forehead with the back of his hand.

"You must be thirsty," Meemaw says.

Beck groans. "Not now, June. You have an appointment in an hour."

"That's plenty of time for"—she squints her eyes at the embroidered patch on the delivery man's brown shirt—"Jarrod here to have a glass of freshly squeezed lemonade."

Jarrod licks his lips and looks nervously from Beck to Meemaw. "Only if it's not too much trouble, ma'am. But I sure am thirsty."

"We don't have much time," Beck interjects, checking his watch.

"A glass of lemonade doesn't take too much time."

"June," Beck says sternly, and I see him slipping into his role as a physician again instead of the man he is when he's with me. "You're delaying on purpose."

"Here," I break in. "Meemaw, I'll get Jarrod the lemonade while you all figure out how to *not* unload one hundred eighteen cast-iron skillets from the truck."

I disappear to the kitchen, leaving Meemaw, Beck, and Jarrod murmuring about pans and logistics behind me. I haven't updated Matt in a while, so I send him a quick text.

Brooke

Meemaw's appointment is today. Did Mom tell you?

Matt responds almost immediately.

Matt

Call me when you're done. How are you doing?

My twin brother might be the world's biggest idiot at times, but I love him, and I know that no one will ever know me quite like he does. And it's not like he doesn't care about Meemaw either.

Brooke

Ok. How's Melanie?

Matt

Amazing. How's your hottie doctor?

Brooke

Ew. Don't call men hotties, Matt. It's weird. Also, he's great.

Matt

Yeah, I know, he called me.

The phone slips out of my hand as I reach for a glass and thumps onto the table.

"Everything ok in here?" Beck's deep voice asks from behind me.

It's my turn to startle. The glass drops to the floor. It's only lightning-fast reflexes honed from years of being determined to beat Matt in everything that allow me to catch it before it hits the ground and shatters.

"Uh … yeah." I stumble over my words a little.

Why would Beck call Matt?

"Why'd you call Matt?" I blurt.

Beck's brow creases, and he chews his lip a little. "I wanted to know if it was ok … if …" He sighs. "I just wanted them to know about me from me, not from June's post."

"Oh. Thank you."

"Of course, Brooke." He brushes my hair behind my ear. "I want to do this right."

"I want to do it right too." I bite my lip, then turn away from Beck's warm gaze to deliver the lemonade.

38

BECK

I shift the truck into park in the dusty lot next to the rehab center I "rescued" June from after her surgery. Brooke and June climb out, and Brooke holds June's hand as we all cross the pavement to the office building.

June stops for a moment, takes a deep breath, and squares her shoulders before stepping into the revolving door with determination. Brooke's steps falter at the door as well, but I give her an encouraging nod, and she follows her grandmother into the building.

The waiting room is all tacky chairs, posters about memory loss, and outdated magazines, but I know the specialist is highly recommended.

"June MacCord," a nurse in sky-blue scrubs calls over a clipboard from her sentinel position in the door to the exam rooms.

"That's me," June says, standing.

Brooke stands too, but I stay seated.

"Aren't you coming too?" Brooke asks.

I shake my head no. "No, I'll stay here. Unless Miss June wants me to come."

We both look to June.

"Of course I want you to come. Who else could make sense of that doctor mumbo jumbo he's about to unleash on me? All these doctory places are the same. Full of people who just don't talk plain English. It's not even Spanish. I've been watching some shows in Spanish just to practice, and doctor lingo isn't even close to any *real* language."

June's here.

"I'll only come back if you promise to be one hundred percent honest with Dr. Arkin."

June crosses her heart. "On my honor." She's using humor, but I see the way her throat tightens and the way she shoves fear down.

Brooke clasps her hands in front of her and fidgets.

"Okay. Who's coming back?" the nurse asks. "Is it all of you?"

"Yes," June declares. "It's all of us."

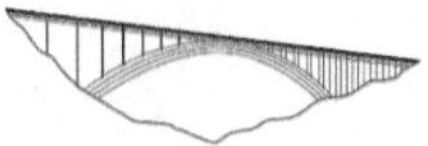

"Well, you two?" June says from around her celebratory ice cream cone. "Now that you have good news about me, what are you going to do with the rest of your day?"

Brooke stops licking her double fudge, double scoop cone with hot fudge, and stares at me.

I set my cup of mint chocolate chip ice cream on the green plastic table.

"I have an idea," I say, pulling out my phone and texting my friends. I am fully aware that Logan will hate me for this, but also that it will be fun.

A drip of chocolate falls off Brooke's cone and plops onto her shirt. "Oh…"

"Whatever it is, Brooke, you should do it," June says. "You only love once, right?"

"Meemaw." Brooke rolls her eyes. "It's you only *live* once."

"That's what I said." June's eyes sparkle with mischief.

"Who said anything about love?" Brooke asks, narrowing her eyes at June.

"I think you two did," June says before taking a huge bite of her strawberry scoop. She says something else, but it's unintelligible with the amount of food in her mouth.

My phone buzzes from where I left it.

Logan

Seriously, man? What did I ever do to you?

I choke down a laugh before I respond.

Beck

That's a yes, then?

Ben

Meet you in an hour.

Brooke's eyes are fixed on my face when I look up from my phone.

"I've got an afternoon planned, if you're up for it." I smile at Brooke while June nods approvingly.

"What is it?" Brooke asks.

"Would you like it to be a surprise?"

Brooke shudders. "No. I do not like unplanned activities. I need to *know* what I'm getting into."

"Would you like to go rafting?"

"Rafting, like floating? Or rafting, like rapids?"

"Logan and Ben will be with us, too, so white water rapids."

Brooke frowns. "But is it safe?"

"Can you swim?"

"Yes."

"Then it's safe enough."

Brooke fidgets with her ice cream cone before she draws in a huge breath. "Ok."

"Excellent," June says, having finally swallowed her bite of dessert. "Now that I know I am experiencing only memory loss related to age, I'm going to call every person who's ever offended me and tell them so. It seems like a good way to keep the old brain sharp."

"Meemaw…" Brooke groans. "He said *crossword puzzles* and *sudoku*, that sort of thing. Not … please don't really do that. Please let some things go."

"Starting with…" June cackles. "My granddaughter who didn't even invite her friends over for lemonade and let me give them unsolicited parenting advice."

"Paige and Connor?" Brooke asks. "You wanted to meet them? They were only here for two nights, and she wasn't feeling very well…"

"I promise I'll make up for it and give you as much parenting advice as you don't want when your time comes. Now, you have a hot date to get to."

The way June's sassy streak is back in full force causes a laugh to bubble up from my chest. A trip to the specialist resulting in *good* news was apparently just what she needed to amplify the more ridiculous parts of her personality. Now that I know more about June, about her kindness, her refusal to bow to social norms she thinks are silly, and her determination to live her life fully, I understand that this woman is admirable. She's not just my annoying neighbor. The doctor assured June that her memory lapses were simply typical for her age. He also suggested that while she has all her faculties, she tours assisted living facilities in case she does need help in the future.

June didn't even bat an eye at that. "I think I'd like a place next to a restaurant so if the food's bad one day, I can get out and eat something real."

Dr. Arkin quirked an eyebrow at me while I sat in the hard plastic chair and held Brooke's hand. Brooke hid her giggle behind her other hand, but after holding space for the stress and worry of the two women it turns out I care most about in the world, the moment went from heavy to lighthearted, and I couldn't be happier about it.

After June gave Dr. Arkin several more comments, including that he should consider putting his office as far away from the unconstitutional jailers at the post-surgery rehab center next door as possible, we left.

I'm not a sentimental man—it's not in my DNA—but my dad always believed in celebrating good news with ice cream, and I couldn't let this moment pass. When I turned into Angie's Angel Ice Cream and Frozen Treats, June clapped her hands like a little girl, and I knew I'd made the right choice.

Now, watching June and Brooke banter back and forth, and feeling the sun beat down on my neck, something in my heart clicks into place. I'm part of a family. Not one with a vindictive and controlling mother and a father who never had the energy to stand up to her after working demanding hours at his construction company, and then died when I was young. I'm part of a family I *want* to be a part of.

"So," Brooke says, addressing me. "What does one wear while rafting with locals? I've seen what the tourists wear, but I have a feeling rafting with Logan when he's *not* working might be different."

Brooke's question makes me think of the flotation devices my not-medically-minded friends would rather *not* wear. "Uh ... I guess I should have asked. Are you a *good* swimmer? Have you ever swam in rough water?"

"Yes. I grew up on Lake Superior."

That means nothing to me, but June nods like it's impressive. "She's more than a good swimmer, she used to compete and beat everyone."

"Meemaw…" Brooke gives her a scathing look. "Sorry, I'm pretty strong at swimming, but Meemaw thinks my eighth-grade gold championship medal in the 200-meter freestyle is impressive."

I snort. "First place is always impressive."

"I was thirteen. That was over a decade ago."

June waves her hand like it doesn't matter. "Once you're good at something, you don't just become ungood at it."

"How much of an adventure are you up for, Brooke?" I ask.

"Probably not the Upper Gauley," she says. "Logan showed me a video of Gauley Season, and that is insanity."

I bite my tongue. I've *done* Gauley Season, but yes, it absolutely is insanity for someone who's never rafted. "Let's keep it easy and fun."

Logan will think it's a waste of time, but I'll enjoy it, I'll be with Brooke.

39

BROOKE

Beck drove Meemaw and me back home after our ice cream and instructed me to grab a swimsuit, shorts, and a shirt that could get wet. I knew I needed all that and closed-toe shoes from the checklist at work, but I still feel a little concerned that if I'm not going on a paid tour, something crazy is going to happen.

My fingers find their way into my hair again.

Meemaw watches me as I collect everything I need. "Honey," she calls out. "Do you really not trust him still?"

I frown and sit in the kitchen chair next to her. "What do you mean?"

"Your hair, Brookie." She gently reaches out a hand and pulls my hand away from my roots. "Is *trust* why you always like to be the one who plans everything?"

I swallow. Grandmotherly wisdom I don't want to hear is forthcoming.

"You know that you can trust him. And his friends. And the people here. You know that. So let go a little, Brookie, and enjoy the adventure. You don't have to control everything."

My mouth drops open.

Beck knocks on the front door and then lets himself in. My mouth still hangs open from Meemaw's wisdom, but when my eyes turn to Beck, my jaw would have dropped anyway.

He wears a black Dri-FITshort-sleeve shirt and black swim trunks with tiny classic cars printed all over, but if that wasn't enough, the black baseball cap with the WVU School of Medicine perched backward on his head would have done me in.

Beck dresses casually, despite being a doctor, but I've never seen him look like this.

He blinks his brown eyes at me a few times, and I shake my head to clear the shock of how attractive he is even in this attire. Meemaw laughs.

"Doctor got your tongue, Brookie?" she needles, then adds in a low voice, "I'm sure he will before the day is out."

"Meemaw!" I hiss while Beck snickers. I'm glad Beck knows Meemaw's a meddlesome woman whose filter disintegrated at least six decades ago, if she ever had one.

"Ready?" Beck asks, his eyes twinkling in amusement.

"Yep." I stand up from the chair, and it's Beck's turn to gape. My swimsuit is modest by every stretch of the imagination, but I'm thrilled he clearly finds me attractive in the short-style bottoms and short-sleeved pink top I threw over my bathing suit tank.

"No babies yet, you two," Meemaw says, and Beck shakes his head before smiling.

"I know, I know, Miss June. Rings first, babies later."

He extends a hand to me, and I take it.

Beck doesn't drive us to the RAFT headquarters. Instead, he drives us along the New River until we reach a secluded turn-off from the road tucked into a copse of Virginia pines.

"I thought we'd meet at work," I say as Beck switches the ignition off.

"Nah. This is where the locals put in."

I take in the empty gravel lot. "But where are the others?"

An old SUV and a newer truck pulling off the road drown out my question. Logan and Ben hop out of the older SUV, but the blue truck catches my attention.

I pause for a moment and then run to it.

Matt opens the door.

"Matt!" I shout and launch at my twin in a bear hug. "How did you end up here? What are you doing? Why didn't you tell me you were coming?" I can't help it, I'm speaking in twin.

Matt squeezes me back and then steps out of my embrace. "Melanie and I came down to visit and see how you're doing." He doesn't speak in twin, and I'm upset about it for a moment, but then I turn and catch sight of Melanie, who stands shyly off to the side in a bright blue one-piece. "And this guy named Logan called us and asked us if we'd like to come rafting with you and your boy."

"My boy?"

He nods. "His words, not mine."

I catch Logan smiling bemusedly from beside Beck and Ben as he fills up a raft with an air pump. He hands the pump to Ben and hops over the partially inflated raft as Ben takes over.

"Did we surprise you?" he asks as he crosses the lot to me. "I've heard you hate them, but this seemed like a good one."

"I don't hate surprises. I just don't prefer them," I retort. "And yes, you did, and I'll accept this surprise."

"Good," Logan says before he turns his blindingly white smile on Melanie. "Hey, I'm Logan. You ever been white water rafting before?"

"Twice," Melanie replies, surprising me. Maybe my assumption she's a shrinking violet was wrong.

"Awesome. This is going to be just for fun, and this isn't a commercial run, so let's do it."

Ben and Beck pick up the inflated raft and carry it to the river bank. Beck jumps into the water and holds the raft steady as the water laps at his shins.

Ben returns to the old SUV and grabs helmets from the back seat before shouting, "Hey, everyone, come grab your helmets and PFDs." He puts the helmet on the ground and directs the next part of his speech toward the water. "I'd rather not wear these, but *someone* insisted. Apparently brain injuries are an E.R. doctor's nightmare."

I have to laugh at Ben's commentary, clearly meant for Beck.

Beck shouts back, "You'll be thanking me when they save your life, man."

"Don't come at me with the helmet on a motorcycle garbage again," Ben yells back before he lowers his voice and says to me, "Your boy used to be the wildest of us all. Now, he won't even let us think about doing something dangerous without safety gear."

My eyebrows hike up my forehead as I place my helmet on.

"Really?" I ask, glancing toward the water where Beck holds the raft patiently. I hold my orange life jacket by the straps. "He was wild?"

"Oh … the stories I could tell you." He tips his head toward Beck. "But I think he'd rather tell you. Maybe you should ask him about the time we—"

"Are you coming, or am I just going to stand here all day holding onto this boat?" Beck yells.

Ben smirks at me before pulling a stack of brightly colored paddles out of the back seat and holding them up across his body like a drilling soldier. "Ask him about his college days, Brooke. I think you'll be pleasantly surprised that our doctor Beckett Whistler isn't the uptight man he seems to be."

I take a moment to digest this news. What could Beck have been like as a college student, a teen, and a little boy? I don't know a lot about his past, except that he was in a serious relationship with Addie, and then she left him at the altar. And his sister made him despise snakes. Somehow, the calm and reserved man in the water has my heart, and somehow, even though I don't know all of his past, I know enough about the present to know he's good. And enough about his friends that a wild streak makes perfect sense.

With nothing else to do to prepare for the trip, I follow Ben to the river. Logan is already there, helmet on his head, but the strap unbuckled at his chin. The jaunty way it sits atop his blond hair makes him look like a movie star in a WWII film. Beck's helmet is secured under his chin, and Matt and Melanie stand on the rocks with their arms around each other's waists, taking a selfie.

"Oh, this is perfect!" Melanie squeals as she clicks the button again, and again, and again, trying a different face with each shot. For the last one, she leans over and plants a kiss on Matt's cheek.

I resist the urge to gag, but just barely. That's my twin brother.

Matt's eyes take in Melanie with such affection, I am immediately transported to a future at their wedding. In this vision, though, I don't sit alone. In fact, I'm not even sitting. In my dream scenario, I'm dancing in the very strong arms of a certain Doctor Beckett Whistler. It's not an unpleasant daydream.

"Everyone good?" Logan calls, pulling me from my daydreams. His demeanor is calm, but I sense that he's ready, and maybe even a little excited about this. "Brooke, you good in the bow?"

I shake my head to clear the mental image away and focus on the task at hand. Beck tips his head to the side as he studies me. I don't know if he can see my thoughts, but when I meet his gaze, he breaks into a grin. It's just *him*, completely at ease in this moment.

His deep voice calls out, "Brooke? You good in the front?" and reminds me I didn't give a response to Logan.

"Sure," I say as I climb over the rocks and stand on the opposite side of the raft from Beck.

"Hop in." Beck raises his chin to indicate the front seat on the left side of the raft.

I start to climb in, and though the water isn't deep, long legs are not something I was genetically gifted. I maintain that Matt stole all the height genes in the womb and have made it my mission to beat him in every competitive event possible since.

I try to hook my leg over the side, but I slip in the water and fall back, landing with a splash on my back.

"Brooke?" Beck's by my side in an instant. I'm completely fine, just a bit shocked to be on my back when, a moment ago, I was trying to mount the raft. Beck's strong arms pull me up so I'm sitting in the river. "Are you ok?" he whispers as his worried eyes scan me for injury.

"Yeah," I say, taking a breath before standing up. Before I stand all the way, I cup my hand under the water and bring it up fast. Water splashes on Beck's neck, and he startles.

When he turns an incredulous gaze toward me, I smile sweetly and begin to clamber into the boat. Unfortunately, it's now even more slippery after my fall.

Matt snickers, and Logan laughs as I slide down the side.

Suddenly, warm hands are on my waist, and I'm hoisted into the boat. It's not dignified, but I slither over the side with the extra help from Beck.

Matt and Melanie sit in the middle, each holding their paddle, and Ben and Logan sit in the back. I adjust my swim shorts and then accept the paddle Matt passes me.

"You better not fall out in the rapids, or you'll never get back in," Matt teases.

I don't say anything, just swing my paddle around so that if he wasn't paying attention, the top part of the oar would whack his helmet. He ducks, and I roll my eyes.

"Hey, no swinging paddles!" Logan calls from the back.

"That rule can't possibly apply to twins," I call back.

"Fair enough, I'd whack Lynette if she was giving me a hard time too. Siblings get a pass on the paddle rule."

Ben shakes his head at his friend as Beck pulls the boat into deeper water. In a move entirely too deft for the reserved man I've known, he leans one arm on the edge of the boat and then elegantly jumps in.

40

BECK

I'm not a tall man by any means, but Brooke is definitely short. When she couldn't get into the boat, my first instinct was to laugh at the determined way she approached the physical challenge. That instinct fled and was replaced by the worry that always accompanies people I care about when she fell back into the water. I'm logical. I *know* that the river is shallow here, and that we were by the bank. But also, the moment she went under, my heart plummeted into my stomach (which I know is not physiologically possible, but it still feels real).

When she playfully splashed me, I got a look at a woman who's determined to have fun despite the challenges life throws at her. Having fun is something I've had to work hard to do since everything happened with Addie. But even before that, medical school, residency, and seeing trauma after trauma every night in the E.R. make it hard for me to let go and live a little sometimes. Anxiety masked by gruffness and irritation became my coping mechanism. Brooke's anxiety is different. She's got big feelings, but she's not afraid. She leans *in* to things, where I lean *out*.

I find myself wanting to impress her, so even though I haven't approached something like recreational white water rafting with my friends with this level of enthusiasm since I was in college, I swing myself into the boat like I'm a regular Indiana Jones.

When Logan passes me a paddle and instructs everyone to put on their life jackets, I don't miss the bemused look he shoots my way. I shrug, rolling my shoulders like that's a totally normal move for me to make. At one time, it was. For the past four years, it has *not* been.

"Beck's back." Ben whistles.

Brooke's eyes search my face while I just shrug. Logan shouts out simple directions, but the truth is, he could do this section of the river on his own and be fine.

We make it over the first set of Class III rapids with no problem, but when we approach the second, I see exactly what he's doing. Logan's aiming to unseat as many people as possible in the boat—himself excluded, of course. We hit the whitewater, and the raft cuts into the rapids, spinning around and drenching everyone on my side of the boat.

Logan shouts instructions from the back, but I can't hear him over the roar of the water. It's a good thing Logan, Ben, and I have done this so many times because Matt is clutching his paddle in shock while Melanie furiously paddles like her life depends on it. No wonder we're spinning.

We're out of the rapids in a minute, thanks to Ben and I righting the spinning ship.

"So," Brooke says once we've all taken a breath. "You used to be wild?"

I grimace. "Past tense there is pretty crucial."

"So you've done this before?"

I bob my head. I've done more than this before. I've rafted the Upper Gauley with Logan during Gauley season. A feat I do not recommend to anyone except the most experienced of rafters.

"Interesting." She studies me, then whistles, loud and shrill. "Logan! Give us some actual directions this time!"

Logan's laughter floats on the breeze as he shouts instructions for the next set of rapids, still Class III, but a little more technical.

The white water sloshes over the boat as everyone tries to follow Logan's calls. It's not effective, and Melanie whoops before hanging onto my shoulder to stay in the raft. Although I had good balance, the extra weight throws me off-kilter, and I'm pitched out of the boat. I have a moment of panic when I hear Brooke scream my name, but the truth is, I grew up on this river, and I know what to do. It's probably in my DNA.

I swim to the side of the river, letting the current carry me downstream to the next stretch of calm water. I manage to get there before the boat, so I wait, treading water. I take a moment to watch the people on the raft as it comes close enough that I can see everyone's faces. Logan's is not the jolly good time face he usually wears, Ben's is stricken, and Melanie and Matt don't say anything. But it's Brooke's face that clues me into what they think happened.

Brooke's eyes are huge as she searches from side to side, looking everywhere along the river. She didn't see me swim away; she only saw me go under.

"Hey!" I shout. "Hey, I'm ok."

All the heads in the boat snap toward me.

"Get back in this boat, you…" Ben growls, and I know he has several colorful words he'd like to use but is refraining from since there are ladies present.

I swim over, and Ben reaches out to help me get back in. I'm dripping and a little cold in the air, but Brooke grabs my hand when I pass. As soon as I sit down, she launches herself into my arms and wraps me in a hug.

"I thought you'd drowned," she whispers against my shoulder while I rub soothing circles on her back.

"It would take more than that to do me in, love," I whisper back, forgetting where we are and who we're with.

When I look up, I find four faces gaping at me. Logan and Ben knew I loved Brooke, but I don't think they anticipated how deep I'd jumped in. Hint, guys: forever.

Matt breaks the silence first. "Love?"

Melanie frowns as she turns toward Matt. "Some men don't have commitment issues, apparently." She flips her hair over her shoulder.

Logan and Ben look at each other for a brief moment before looking back at me. Ben raises his eyebrows, but Logan frowns.

"Uhh. Yes?" I say to Matt. "I know we haven't spent much time together, but what did you think it meant when I called to tell you I was dating your sister and that I wanted to know you better?"

"I don't know," Matt sputters. "But I didn't think it meant you were already in *love* terrain."

Brooke lets go of me and turns to face her twin. I can't understand everything she says because she says it rapid fire, and I think it's nonsense, but Matt shrinks back from her fury.

"Ok, sorry," he says, holding his hands up. "Mel, I … don't say those words until I mean them."

"Then what am I even doing with you?" Melanie snaps.

Strange things happen on this river, but witnessing a couple fight in between rapids has to be the strangest thing I've ever seen.

"Melanie," Brooke cuts in. "Matt is the taller twin, not the smarter one. He might not have told you it yet, but he clearly loves you. You're the only girl he's dated for longer than a week in…" She closes her eyes and ticks off her fingers. "Ever."

Melanie's delicate eyebrows draw into sharp carats above her nose. "Really?" she asks as she swipes the back of her hand across her eyes. Mascara runs down her cheeks.

"Really," Matt says, which results in Melanie throwing herself on Matt for a lengthy kiss.

Brooke averts her eyes after whispering, "Ewww."

Logan and Ben look at each other, and then Ben calls, "Nope," and dives out of the boat.

"Ugh. Can I join him?" Brooke asks, looking longingly at the water. "This is indecent."

"I think they love each other," I say in a low voice.

"Yeah, but he's my *brother*."

I adopt a faux psychiatrist demeanor. "Does that make you uncomfortable?"

Brooke snorts and I lower my voice to a conspiratorial whisper. "I think in this instance, payback could be fun."

Logan rolls his eyes, but Brooke's blue ones sparkle with mischief.

"What do you have in mind?" she asks as she takes the flat edge of the paddle and pokes Matt with it. "Matt!" she hollers.

Matt swats the paddle away, but Brooke keeps poking him with it. This stretch of river is calm. There's still a few more rapids, but for now, we can swim. Or perhaps a better thought would be *they* can swim.

Logan knows exactly what I'm suggesting when he catches my eye. We've done this a time or two, usually to him and whatever girl he's picked up for the day. "Too much love happening in this boat today," he grumbles, but then hops to the seat right behind Melanie and Matt and plops down with just enough force to catapult them into the water. Coupled with my own well-timed stumble where I 'accidentally' bump into Matt's shoulder, the two love birds pop out of the boat and splash into the water.

"H-hey!" Melanie sputters indignantly as they surface.

"You did that on purpose!" Matt accuses as he shakes a fist at us.

Logan quirks a brow in plausible denial, and my part of payback for Matt and his makeout is to pull Brooke into my arms and kiss her.

"Gross! That's my sister!" Matt shouts from the water.

I break my kiss with Brooke. "That's the point!" I call back.

"Ok, lovers," Logan shouts. "It's time to get back to the boat because we've got our Class IV rapids coming up around this bend."

41

BROOKE

Matt and Melanie swim back to the boat, and Ben's head appears on the other side of the raft. Logan and Beck extend hands to Melanie and haul her in, where she sits dripping wet but weirdly glowing because, apparently, my twin brother loves her. Weird. And gross. I can't contemplate too much about that because Ben hops into the boat, swinging his legs over like he's a gymnast on a pommel horse.

Matt's reentry is not nearly as smooth as Ben's or Beck's, and does it make me a terrible sister if that fills me with a tiny bit of glee? More teasing ammo is always a good thing when you have a twin, so no. Not terrible.

Matt grabs his paddle. "What do we need to do, boss?" he directs at Logan before winking at Melanie.

Beck catches my side eye and mouths, "You ok?"

I nod back, listening while Logan tells us about how we'll be approaching this rapid. He's more serious than he has been before, and his instructions reflect that. We have a few moments of paddling before we round the bend, so I drop my voice to a low whisper and ask Beck, "What's their story?" I tip my head to indicate Ben and Logan.

Beck gives a watery sort of smile and shakes his head. I can tell he isn't saying he won't tell me, just that now isn't the right time for that conversation. If the mark of a man is the company he keeps, Logan and Ben are definitely interesting company, and I'd like to know their stories. Mainly why Logan keeps frowning at Matt and Melanie, and why Ben dove out of the boat when they started locking lips.

The rapids hit right after the curve in the river, and there's a moment of hushed concentration as the boat twists around the bend. Beck, Logan, and Ben know this river. It's clear from the way they've approached the entire afternoon of fun, but even they tighten the grip on their paddles and face this rapid with an uncharacteristic seriousness.

As soon as we're in the rough water, I understand why.

"Back two! Back two!" Logan hollers as Beck begins paddling backward twice. "Four! Four!" Logan shouts again.

I attempt to paddle, but the rapids are buffeting the boat, and my side of the boat is popped up in air above them, so my paddle doesn't even dip into the river. I'm paddling *air*. My stomach swoops as the nose of the boat tips under the surface, and spray flies into my eyes, my ears, and my open mouth. Somehow, I don't lose my paddle in the chaos as Logan continues to shout different numbers.

"Three! Three!" he yells over the roar, and this time, when I start to stroke, the paddle slices into the water.

It might be only a few minutes, but it feels like much longer before the raft slips out of the white water and into the calmly flowing river again. My heart ran a marathon in just a short expanse of river, and I take a deep breath as the raft lazily slides along. I let it out shakily. It's not enough to still my racing heart, so I do it again. As I inhale, I catch Beck watching me with concerned eyes. It's enough to completely undo the calm that was starting.

"Have fun?" he asks.

"Y-yeah," I say. "That was a lot more wild than I thought it would be."

Beck turns to face the back of the boat. "Hey, is Lynette picking us up?"

"Yep, in about twenty minutes," Logan calls back and then tips his head to the river.

"Anyone up for a swim?" Beck asks before setting his paddle down and gracefully jumping over the side.

"I think I'd rather stay in the boat this time," Melanie says to Matt.

I set down my paddle and attempt to exit the inflatable boat as gracefully as Beck. Again, my short legs don't let me leap over the wall of air-filled plastic, and my skin makes a slapping sound as it hits the wet material before I slide off the raft and into the water.

"I'll hold the boat at the next shallow spot," Logan calls as he passes by us with Matt and Melanie still in the middle. Just when the boat clears us, Ben stands at the edge of the back and falls purposefully backward into the river, where he lands with a huge splash.

"Sooo, Brooke," Ben says as he floats over to me. "How's your grandma's car?"

"Oh, it's fine," I say, looking around the water for Beck. My heart is in my throat because I can't see him.

Suddenly, something pulls on my leg, and I kick it, shrieking. Beck's copper hair breaks the surface of the water, and he grins at me. It's an actual grin, a playful one, the kind where he doesn't look like the weight of saving lives is pressing down on him. The seriousness usually present in his posture is gone.

"Are. There. Snakes. In. Here?" I ask, looking around, even though I know it was Beck that grabbed my leg.

Beck shrugs. "Probably, but I wouldn't worry about it. The rapids wouldn't be good for them." He swims closer to me and loops a finger around my life jacket strap. "Are you scared?"

I shudder at the idea of snakes. "Definitely."

"Did we just find someone who likes snakes even less than you?" Ben asks, surfacing on my other side.

"Doubtful," Beck responds as I say, "Absolutely" at the same time.

Ben's eyes twinkle with a knowing light. "Well, I've heard that snakes are romantic."

Beck's gaze snaps to Ben. "Don't you dare use Bea's lines on me."

Beck splashes water at Ben, but Ben ducks behind his hand before laughing.

"One day, we'll get her to bring a python or maybe a boa constrictor and leave it in your bed."

Beck smirks. "That's illegal, thank goodness. And I happen to know you don't want to live a life of crime."

"For the record, I'll have no part in this prank," I say.

Beck pulls me a little closer and wraps an arm around my life jacket girth before he leans in. He plants a brief kiss on my temple that makes a warmth linger on my skin against the coolness of the water.

"Not a life of crime," Ben corrects, "but if Bea asked me to help her prank you like that, I would."

"Threatening me, Benjy?" Beck questions, a glint in his eye.

"Of course I am," Ben says back. "That's what friends do. Right, *Becky*?"

Beck lets go of my life jacket and begins chasing down Ben, who clearly anticipated this because he is booking it down the river as fast as he can go. I swim after them, not wanting to be left behind because now I'm thinking about snakes, and that is a hard pass for me.

Beck overtakes Ben, and the two of them start good-naturedly wrestling in the water. I'm glad to have grown up with brothers, because the entire thing doesn't strike me as odd at all.

But Melanie must not have grown up with brothers because she's shrieking from the boat. "Stop! Matty, stop them! They're going to get hurt!"

I forget for a moment to tread water because I'm so incredulous at her overreaction. My head bobs under the water, and I force myself back up only to find that Logan and Matt stare at Melanie slack-jawed while Beck and Ben continue trying to shove one another under the water. It's difficult in life jackets.

I swim to the shallow area where Logan has let the raft bump up against a boulder.

"They're just playing, Mel," Matt says as I pop my head over the side of the raft.

I reach my hand out to try to pull myself over the wall, but I can't, so Logan helps me in.

"That's barbaric," Melanie says, shuddering.

I slump onto a seat and turn to see that Beck has pushed Ben under, but at the last second, Ben pops up and pushes Beck under. I know how this goes. I put two fingers in my mouth and whistle at the loudest, shrillest decibel I can.

Beck and Ben break apart and turn toward the boat.

"Boys," I say, putting my hands on my hips, although it's difficult over the personal flotation device. "That's enough."

"Yes, ma'am," Beck calls back, laughing with Ben.

"Our ride's picking us up in ten, so everyone back in," Logan yells.

Beck and Ben look at each other for a half beat before they launch into a race, swimming as fast as they can over to us. When they get to the raft, they both swing in like they're some sort of water cowboys.

Beck situates himself across the boat from me, and when he catches my eye, it's the unbridled joy in his gaze that has me feeling like I'm about to go over a Class V rapid.

42

BECK

Lynette picks us up from just before the bridge in one of Logan's family's company buses.

"So," Lynette says once we're all situated. "Who's going to the dance tomorrow?"

Melanie immediately perks up. "Dance?"

Logan releases a sigh. "Lynette. C'mon, you know better."

"Whoopsies," she says, sounding not sorry at all.

"Dance?" Brooke asks me, her tone much quieter than Melanie's.

I knock my knee into hers on the bench seat as I grab her hand. "Billy's holds a dance every September for the locals. They keep it quiet because they don't want it to become a tourist attraction. If you come with a local, then you can get in, but it's not something they advertise."

"Oh." Brooke's shoulders slouch a little.

"You do know that you're a local now, right?" I ask.

"I am?" Brooke brightens, then, like a flash, it's gone. "I guess I am."

"Can we go?" Melanie blinks big brown eyes at me. "You're a local, and I'd love to go to a dance. Wouldn't you, Matt?"

"Uh…" Matt flounders.

"It's very, very casual," Ben cuts in. "Like line-dancing-in-your-boots casual."

Melanie frowns, but at the words *line dancing*, she perks back up. "That sounds fun. Can we go? Can we?"

Matt looks at Logan, who's scowling at Lynette, and then at me. "I think we need someone to vouch for us."

Brooke swallows. "I'd like to go to the dance. But only if I'll know someone there."

I bite back a laugh at her obvious attempt to find out if I'm going. I slide my arm around her shoulder and pull her close to my side. "Would you like to go to the dance with me, Brooke?"

She turns wide, serious blue eyes my way and nods.

"Can we come too?" Melanie's head pops up over the seat in front of us. "You said if there are locals with you, then us *lame* tourists get to come, right?"

"Yes," I say, keeping my voice measured. I happen to know that the owner of Billy's isn't going to like me bringing along *any* tourists, but there's no way I can say no to Brooke's twin's girlfriend. "But you should know that there are some expectations for everyone who attends."

"Oh, like what?"

"No filming for social media," Logan butts in. "You're an influencer, right?"

Indignation flashes across her face before she sits a little taller. "Content creator. How did you know that?"

"I can always tell," Logan mutters under his breath.

"And if you show up with a non-local, as a non-local, the local guys are going to try stuff," Ben interjects.

"Well, that sounds interesting!" Melanie chimes in. She squeezes Matt's bicep. "Matt can take them, right?"

Matt has muscles. Matt owns a gym. Matt is a personal trainer. And yet, Matt is *not* going to be able to take some of the guys if they all decide to gang up on him.

"Oh, c'mon, guys," Lynette calls from the wheel. "You know you're all going, so it will be fine."

Lynette is seven years younger than me, Ben, and Logan. She's got a year left of college. She wasn't old enough to go to the dance six years ago, but I was, and I saw the way some of the local troublemakers got into it with the tourist couple who happened to wander in. Addie was involved in riling everyone up, and eventually fists flew.

I don't think Melanie will do what Addie did, and I know Brooke won't. I promised her I would remember that she isn't Addie. Even though I haven't had any interest in dancing with anyone in years, a night with Brooke in my arms sounds heavenly.

I blow out a breath. "Ok," I say. "Logan, Ben, will you guys be coming too?"

"Yes!" Lynette pipes up. "Girls, this is going to be so much fun! Let's go shopping!"

"You're coming?" Logan sputters.

"Uhh, yeah. I'm twenty-one now."

Matt, Melanie, and Brooke watch the exchange with their heads on a swivel.

"Great, now I have to go," Logan moans. "Ben, you better come with me."

"Don't you have a date?" I quip.

"Not when my sister's going to Billy's, I don't."

"This is going to be so much fun!" Lynette squeals before taking a hairpin turn too fast and grazing the side of the bus against the mountain wall. Brooke's hand shoots out and latches onto my forearm, and she squeezes tightly. The bus rights itself, but she doesn't release her hold.

"Is this safe?" Brooke whispers, her voice riddled with anxiety.

"Probably," I whisper back, trying to lighten the mood a little as I tighten my arm around her shoulder. Brooke closes her eyes in response and exhales shakily before she leans her head on my shoulder. It's perfect.

"This might have been too much excitement for one day for me," she murmurs.

"Yeah," I say in return, before I press a kiss to her forehead, "but you get to go to a dance, and I think you get to go shopping with Lynette and Melanie if you want to."

Lynette turns the bus into the gravel lot where we left our cars and parks.

"Girls?" she says as she stands up from the driver's seat. "Want to go shopping tomorrow?"

Melanie shouts, "Yes!" as Brooke shakes her head 'no'.

Matt fixes Brooke with a look, and some non-verbal telepathic twin communication passes between them.

Brooke rolls her eyes at Matt before pasting on a smile and responding, "Sure. Let's go shopping."

43

BROOKE

It's the day of the dance, one day after our rafting adventure, and I can now attest that Lynette's fun. She's quirky and smart. Melanie and Lynette talk the entire ride to the store. Melanie hops into the front seat, and Lynette's driving, so I'm tagging along in the back like some kind of human-shaped third wheel.

I like shopping. But it was clear from the moment Lynette and Melanie stepped foot in the door of the shop that they had very different ideas of what one wears to a dance and that I was going to be in the crosshairs of their very vocal opinions.

When we finally get to the store and are perusing the stacks of neatly folded jeans in a gradient of blue colors, Lynette broaches something. "So, you're an influencer?" she says to Melanie, eyes wide. "Maybe I could do that."

Melanie eyes Lynette up and down. "Content creator. And you could." She says it in such a gracious and encouraging way that I'm surprised. It's not what I've come to expect from girls who look like her. "You'd need a niche, though. What would you do?"

Lynette bites her lip, her eyes roving around until they meet mine. "I think maybe psychology and hiking. Maybe … hike the Appalachian Trail."

"Ooh, that could work. You definitely have the aesthetic for it."

I resist the urge to shake my head. Being an influencer sounds like a terrible idea to me. I like my digital scrapbook, but I don't like my whole life to be out in public for the world to see.

Before I can say anything about it, Melanie lets out a squeal. "Oh. My. Gosh." She runs to the display. "This is *the one* for you, Brooke."

My eyes follow her to a mannequin wearing an exquisite dress. It's chiffon with elbow-length sleeves, a dropped waistline, and the outer fabric is covered in tiny pink rosebuds while the lining is a soft taupe. The entire effect is light and airy and gorgeous.

"It's beautiful," I say, scanning for a dress on the hanger that matches the dress on the mannequin. No luck—this dress is not in sight.

"It's perfect for your complexion and your height, and Beckett is going faint when he sees you in it."

"I'd rather he didn't," I say, standing on my tiptoes to try to see where these beautiful dresses are hidden. "But there aren't any here."

Lynette and Melanie turn, surveying the store.

"What size are you?" Melanie asks.

I answer, and Melanie pulls the tag up from the mannequin's back. "This one is your size. Problem solved."

I blink. "Are you proposing we take the dress off the mannequin?"

Melanie smiles. "Don't you want to wear this dress?"

Lynette giggles behind her hand. "I haven't seen Beck be into anyone in years. I don't think he'll care what you wear, but this dress will definitely knock him out."

Ugh. This dress. It's calling to me like a siren song.

"Shouldn't we ask a store clerk?" I ask.

But Melanie has already unzipped the back of the dress and is sliding it off the mannequin. "They want you to spend your money, not worry about their displays," she chides.

"What if it's not for sale?" I whisper, anxiety flaring.

Lynette holds the cuff of the dress and points to the price tag. "It is for sale, Brooke, and it is about to be yours."

Melanie slips it off the mannequin and hands it to me. "Isn't it indecent to leave the mannequin naked?" I ask her in a hushed voice, not totally convinced we haven't just broken some major rule of clothing stores.

"Brooke," Melanie says before she whips a tiny phone stand and her phone from her pocket. "Go try that dress on in the dressing room. I promise, I will make this all better."

Lynette grabs a pair of jeans and a gauzy green button-down shirt with a high collar that ties together in a scarf. It's not something I'd wear, but she's confident, and who am I to judge? She's the local.

"C'mon, Brooke," Lynette says. "Let's go try these things on and make sure they fit."

We head to the dressing room, but before we duck out of the department, Melanie has already set up her phone on a small tripod and is recording herself redressing the mannequin in an entirely different dress.

"Content," Lynette says, bobbing her head toward Melanie. "She's good."

I have no insight into that, but I'm glad she's not leaving the mannequin naked.

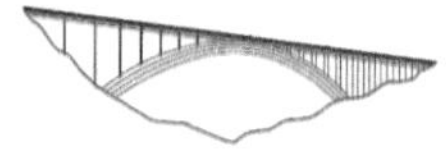

Lynette dropped Melanie and me off at Meemaw's after our shopping excursion. Melanie loops her arm in mine as she carries multiple bags up the porch to Meemaw's house.

"You're back!" Meemaw exclaims as we walk through the door.

Matt's eyes are huge, and he immediately relaxes when he sees Melanie. "Help me," he mouths at me behind Meemaw.

"I was just telling Matthew here the merits of a good ol'-fashioned wedding," Meemaw says. "I need some grandbabies."

I swallow down a laugh, relieved that Meemaw has moved on to pestering Matt, but also taking a little pity on the poor guy. Meemaw's very traditional views mean that Matt has the couch, and Melanie and I are sharing a room at night. He's in for a very long discussion on the finer points of having fun *after* marriage, and I don't think Melanie's quite comfortable with Meemaw's baby coveting just yet.

"Meemaw," I say, changing the subject for Matt's sake, "I got the cutest dress."

Meemaw's eyes widen. "I must see it."

"When is the dance?" Melanie interjects. "We need to get ready, right?"

"Beck said he'd pick us up at eight," I say. "But it's only four now."

"Oh, honey," Melanie says, patting my hand like you would a child's. "We need *all* that time to get ready."

I blow out a breath because Melanie is determined, and Meemaw is nodding along in agreement. "Yes, you ladies need to take your time and get ready. Don't worry, I'll distract the menfolk so you can knock their socks off." Meemaw pats Matt's leg and leans closer to him, loudly whispering, "I'd like at least ten great-grandchildren."

Matt's eyes widen to comical proportions.

I shrug as Melanie leads me past my two blood relations and to the small pink room we're currently sharing. Melanie isn't someone I'd naturally be friends with, but I'm determined to try for Matt's sake. She is a nice person, and I've judged her for her looks without really getting to know her. I also suspect she knows her way around a getting-ready routine.

When she pulls out an entire hair salon's worth of tools from her suitcase, it appears I was right.

"Let's do this," she says, grabbing a comb—and it would seem I have no choice.

44

BECK

It's seven fifty-seven p.m. I know I said I'd pick them up at eight, but I'm pacing with the feeling of dread that accompanies social interactions where Addie could show up. The annual dance at Billy's isn't a secret, and she'll see Ben leaving. If there's even a whiff of drama, she'll be there.

Anticipation and anxiety are driving me crazy. I slide into my shoes, practical boots with enough comfort to dance, and jam my hands into my jeans pockets as I catch sight of my reflection in the mirror behind the front door. I look good.

The hair gel has made my copper hair tidily messy, the hint of stubble growing in on my jaw makes me look rugged, and the soft flannel shirt popped over a plain black t-shirt fits the part of a dive bar having a locals-only dance.

I take my hands out of my pocket and run them through my hair one last time, trying to get it just right. If anything, it doesn't work, and now a piece sticks up at an awkward angle. I try to force it down, but it's determined to stay up.

My eyes track to the crucifix by my door. I swore I wouldn't date anyone after Addie, but here I am, headed out on a date with June's ruby ring in my pocket. I close my eyes and take a breath, praying that I'll know how to move forward, that something will click into place, and I'll know when it's time.

My phone alarm rings. It's eight.

I could stay here and fight with my hair all evening, or I could go pick up my date. It's an easy choice because all my heart wants is to see Brooke.

I slam my front door shut, hoping to leave the anxiety monster behind.

When I knock on June's door, June answers. Matt sits stiffly on the floral couch, his blue eyes rapidly searching from side to side as if he's looking for an escape route. He's wearing jeans and a bright blue quarter zip with a gym logo on it. The B's in Beast and Bastion flank a horizontal line, giving it the effect of a barbell.

"Beckett," June says. "Just wait right here a moment while the girls finish up." She gestures to the couch, and I sit next to Matt.

"Hey, how's it going, man?" I ask.

Matt starts to say something and then stops. For a moment, I'm concerned he's had a stroke, but then it's my turn to lose focus.

Brooke and Melanie walk down the hallway to the living room, arm in arm. Melanie is pretty enough, sure, but my eyes cannot focus on anything but Brooke.

Her dress shifts and flows in the slight breeze of the fans that June keeps running in the heat of the day. It's light and flowy and ethereal, and also *her*. Tiny pink flowers—roses, I think—are printed all over the dress. The hot pink heels make her stand almost equal to my height. She is, in a word, breathtaking.

Breath-stealing would be more accurate. She has stolen my breath with her beauty, and it takes every ounce of control in my body to snap my jaw shut as I behold her.

"Hi," Brooke says from across the room.

June leans against a doorframe, watching me and Matt as she winks at me.

The gentle lilt of Brooke's voice is enough to snap me into action. I stand and cross the room to her, and honestly, I'm not sure what I intend to do, but June interrupts with, "Be a gentleman, Beckett."

Instead of what I want to do, which is to let my physical attraction for Brooke take over, I stop short and grasp her hand, bringing her knuckles to my lips and pressing a kiss against the rough lines of her skin.

Her breath hitches.

"On my honor, Miss June," I say, "I'll be a gentleman."

June gives a single nod before turning her attention to Melanie and Matt. "Young sir!" she exclaims. "You can do *that* when you're married."

Matt hops away from where he was practically making out with Melanie.

"Sorry, Meemaw," he says in contrition.

Melanie flushes, but then she giggles too.

"Is everyone ready?" I ask.

When everyone affirms that they are, I lead the way to my truck, keeping Brooke's hand tucked in mine.

Because parking at Billy's is difficult on a good day and this dance brings the locals out in droves, I offered to drive. Not to mention the fact that Matt's Michigan license plate would stick out like a sore thumb tonight. He seemed to do the math himself and agreed it might be better for me to drive.

Matt and Melanie squeeze into the back seats of my old truck while Brooke hops into the front. As we drive to Billy's, Melanie keeps up a constant chatter about how excited she is to dance and what her favorite dances were in high school and then at her sorority in college.

Brooke catches my eye and raises her brows at the mention of Melanie's sorority experience. Melanie is nice enough, and the more I get to know her, the more the pieces of who she is make perfect sense. It's not that there's anything wrong with sororities, it's just that it all fits so neatly into the box that is Melanie.

I pull into the dirt space that is Billy's parking lot and try to find a spot among the throng of other double-parked vehicles.

Thoughts of how the women in my truck are so different from each other run rampant. Melanie fits into the parameters of the box I'd expect her to, but Brooke, on the other hand, isn't what I expect. Truthfully, I love that about her. Her take-charge personality isn't because she's controlling, it's because it covers up her anxiety.

Brooke's pink streaks of hair are in some sort of braided crown on her head, while the rest of her blonde hair flows long and loose past her shoulders. She's got her phone in her lap, and when it buzzes, she picks it up and smiles softly.

"What's got you smiling?" I ask after I pull into a spot and cut the engine.

"This." She shows me a picture on her phone. It's a black-and-white sonogram with a white area circled, and text interposed that says "baby."

"It's Paige. She had her appointment, and everything looks good."

I know I'm a doctor, but I have always found it odd that women show pictures of their uteruses to each other with baby news. Must be some uniquely female urge that I don't understand. Despite the fact that it *is* weird to show a picture of your uterus to your friends, I am happy for Paige and Connor. Paige and Connor seem like they'll be great parents—warm, loving, kind. All the things my mom was not.

"Is she feeling better?" I ask.

"I'm not sure, I'll ask her." Brooke types out a message and hits send. "Are you ready to dance?"

"Who's having a baby?" Melanie croons.

"My friends Paige and Connor," Brooke says.

"Wait, really?" Matt interjects. "I haven't kept up with them much, but *really?*"

"Yes, really."

"That's awesome. Connor's a good dude. I wonder if he'd like to do some dad bod training with me."

"Uh. Matt, isn't dad bod *not* the kind of training you do?" Brooke asks.

"Exactly," Matt says. "Dads don't have to buy into the message that they don't have time for themselves just because they've got a baby."

"Who are these people, exactly?" Melanie interjects as she hops out of the truck.

"We worked with them at a summer camp a few years back," Matt supplies. "Connor's a good guy, and I'm happy they finally got together."

"We were both at their wedding," Brooke adds. "Matt got to seat all the little old ladies and collected butterscotch candies."

"Uh … okay." Melanie quirks a brow. "You *like* butterscotch candies?"

"It was a different time in my life, Mel," Matt says, shooting Brooke a stern look over the top of Melanie's head.

The telepathic twin communication has me wondering what more to the story there is, but Brooke clears that up.

"Matt had a crush on Paige when we started working there."

Matt's scowl tells me Brooke knew exactly what she was doing by lobbing that nugget of information into Melanie's ears.

"Yeah, well, that went away when it became obvious she only had eyes for Connor." Matt's eyes narrow at Brooke for a half second before he grins mischievously. "And I'm pretty sure Brooke had a crush on Connor too."

I tip my head to the side and study Brooke. She glares at her brother and shrugs. "Yeah, he's nice and attractive. But like you said, he was meant for Paige, and she was meant for him, so that went away real fast."

That makes sense. I've met Connor. He's a nice guy. Very, *very* tall, and he uses more words than I do, and I suppose he's objectively handsome, but something about Brooke and him doesn't seem right. That crush would have been one-sided and *not* have worked. Like pickles and gummy worms—delicious on their own, but not something you put together. These thoughts are weird, but I'm willing to let them go.

Tired of thinking about Brooke's crush on another man, I turn to her, catch her hand, and smile. While she may have had a crush on Connor, I'm the one who's dancing with her tonight.

45

BROOKE

eck leads me into Billy's, where a large man in a black T-shirt accepts a crisp twenty from Beck's wallet.

"You taking these tourists in?" the man asks in a gruff voice.

"Yep," Beck says, and while he's not unkind, there's an edge to his tone.

"You know the rules?"

"Yep."

"Any trouble and—"

"I'm aware," Beck cuts in, the irritation in his voice biting.

"Fine," the man in black says, but as we pass into the dim bar, his eyes linger a little too long on me, Matt, and Melanie.

To my surprise, Beck doesn't stop in the bar. He takes us across the floor and to a back door with a huge "EMERGENCY EXIT" sign. The door is beat up and partially propped open by a rock. When we shimmy through the crack in the door, my breath is taken away.

Edison lights are strung between poles overhead. A wood plank dance floor shines under them. There's a band of folk artists playing to the side of the dance floor, and the dance floor is packed with men and women of all ages dancing.

Long tables with giant bowls of punch are set against the back of the building, and buckets of ice with bottles and cans of drinks are on tall tables. People mill about everywhere. The men are all wearing various shades of plaid and blue jeans, while the women wear everything from jeans to tiny shorts with heeled cowboy boots and dresses.

"Ok," Beck says to Matt. "You guys go have fun and dance, but don't cause any trouble. And Matt, if someone wants to dance with Melanie, you let them have one line dance."

That seems weird.

Matt frowns, but Beck fixes him with a stern glare.

"If they try anything more, you can cut them off, but it's a community dance, and everyone's dancing with everyone. You already stick out as a tourist. Melanie, you can say no if someone asks you to dance, but it would be better to say yes if someone asks you to line dance. And if it's square dancing, it doesn't matter anyway."

"Oh, does this mean I have to dance with anyone who asks me?" I ask as Matt and Melanie wind their way to an empty spot on the dance floor. Truthfully, anxiety is flaring, and I'm trying to shove it down. I can control it. I am in control.

"Absolutely not." Beck frowns. "You will only be dancing with me."

"Seems hypocritical," I retort.

"Ah, but you and I are both locals." Beck tips his chin. "Local people have privileges at these things."

"Fair enough." I smile and let Beck lead me through the crush of people and take our places in the line.

The dances aren't hard, but line dancing doesn't come naturally to me. Beck seems to know these like the back of his hand, and we're laughing and having a great time. After an hour of line dancing, the band switches to square dancing.

Suddenly the people who were line dancing file off the floor, and a whole new group of people file on.

"Want to try it?" Beck asks.

"Could I watch a few rounds first?" I ask, because truthfully I am tired from an hour of activity, and also, I have never seen square dancing in person.

"Of course," Beck says. "Oh look, there's Ben and Logan."

Logan scowls at Ben's back as Ben heads onto the dance floor with Lynette.

"Well, that's interesting," I whisper to Beck, but he doesn't hear me.

Matt and Melanie stand to the side of the dance floor, under one of the Edison bulbs, and I can see Melanie's foot tapping while Matt looks on at the swirling, whirling dancers with trepidation. If line dancing isn't my thing, it's clear that square dancing isn't Matt's.

Beck and I arrive next to Logan.

"Why do you look like that?" Beck asks, slapping Logan on the shoulder.

He juts his head over to where Lynette and Ben are part of a square. "Lynette asked Ben to dance."

"That's better than her asking the other guys to dance here, right?"

"Yeah." Logan runs his hands through his spiky hair before smirking at Beck. "Hey, Brooke, want to dance?"

Beck scowls, but doesn't answer and looks at me.

"Ha, sorry, no, Logan," I say.

Logan laughs. "Had to try."

The square dance music ends, and the caller announces, "We're going to take a break, and when we come back, it will be time for some canoodling music. That's right, ladies and gents, we'll move on to the love songs after this break."

Ben and Lynette return from the dance floor, holding bottles of beer from the ice bucket. They offer them all around, but I politely decline. "I'm going to head to the bathroom."

Beck nods in understanding. Lynette passes her beer to Ben and says, "I'll come too."

We duck back into the building, and it would appear that every woman had the same idea we did. While we're waiting in line, the band starts playing soft, romantic songs that make me want to somehow both run into Beck's arms and also run away because there is too much anticipation coursing through my body for my brain to have any logical response.

Lynette talks my ear off the entire time we wait, but I don't mind. This is the first year she's been able to come to the dance, and although she doesn't say anything directly, I get the sense she's hoping that Ben will ask her to dance. I don't know how Logan will feel about it, but it's not my business.

When we're finally done and return to the outside, we find the men just as we left them, except Logan's gesticulating wildly, and I catch Ben's words of "too soon." He cuts off abruptly when he sees me.

The band is playing a soft melody that I can't totally place. Beck frowns at Ben and Logan, and before the anxiety runs away, I unleash my take-charge attitude.

"Let's dance!" I say, shoving Lynette lightly toward Ben. She stumbles a little, but Ben catches her, steadying her with his hands on her arms.

Logan stalks off just as Beck extends his hand to me.

"Dance with me?" he asks, which seems redundant because I just said I wanted to dance, but I appreciate it just the same.

I grasp his hand and let him lead me to the floor. For once, it's nice to let someone else lead. The moment his hands set themselves on my waist, any nerves I had about this moment fly away.

Beck is gentle, and kind, and good, and I love the man. I can't help the anxiety about new situations that I routinely shove down and power through, but I can give Beck the gift of trusting him, and I do. I lean into him just as he bends slightly to whisper something in my ear.

My heart swoops low when he quietly sings the lyrics to the song. It's "Can't Help Falling in Love."

I am undone. All I want is to kiss the man, to marry the man, to have a family with the man who's holding me gently in his arms and singing his love for me.

Just as I'm about to tell him this, an extremely unwelcome voice cuts in as someone elbows me out of the way. "That's him. He's the one who brought those tourists."

Addie.

"You said you knew the rules," the bouncer growls. "They're out of here, and so are you."

"Bye, Beckett," Addie says as she tosses her hair over her shoulder.

The man in black grabs Beck's arm and twists it behind his back before he pushes him through Billy's and into the parking lot.

46

BECK

"Billy," I say as he shoves me through the bar. "What on earth did I do?"

"The young lady said the tourists you brought were bothering her. Wouldn't back off when she said she wouldn't dance with him."

I roll my eyes. Matt did *not* ask Addie to dance. This entire thing stinks of vindictive malice. "How much did she pay you?"

"Now, Beckett, you know that I can't be bought," Billy responds.

"How. Much. Did. She. Pay. You?" I grind out, but Billy just flashes a smile, complete with a missing tooth on the left upper row, a result of a bar fight he broke up single-handedly, if his own tall tales are to be believed. Billy is not someone I believe.

Billy pushes me through the front door and gives me a salute before disappearing back into the bar.

I shake out my arm before realizing I left Brooke alone in there.

I don't have to panic for long because Brooke, Logan, and Ben spill out of the front door of Billy's just moments after I start worrying.

"What happened?" Logan asks.

I tell him.

"Well, I'm not staying here on principal," Logan quips. "C'mon, Ben."

Ben shakes his head. "I'll keep an eye on Lynette before Liggly gets to her. He was eyeing her."

Logan gives him a stern nod before Ben disappears back into Billy's.

Matt and Melanie stand with their arms crossed in front of my truck. I head to the two of them.

"What happened, man?" Matt asks. "One second, we were dancing, and the next, we were told we weren't welcome here anymore."

"My ex," I grumble.

Melanie's eyebrows shoot up into her hairline. "That woman. She's … your ex?"

"Uh, yeah. Why?"

"Oh, I just … know her from a few years ago at a conference in California for content creators... She was never very nice."

"That sums it up."

I check my watch—there's still an hour before I had planned to be back at June's. Addie might be trying to ruin my date, but she's not going to ruin my life anymore. I knew it the moment I started singing to Brooke. I can't help it, I'm in love with her, and will be until I die.

That prayer to know when it's time—it was answered when I held her in my arms and a lifetime of love flashed before my eyes.

"Hey, Logan?" I call.

Logan rolls his eyes because he already knows what I'm going to ask, but he owes me.

"Would you take Matt and Melanie back to June's?"

Logan shakes his head. "You sure?"

Beck nods. "Positive."

"I can't talk you out of it?"

"Not a chance."

Logan shrugs. "Then sure." He looks at Matt and Melanie. "There's absolutely no making out in my truck, you two. I let it slide on the boat, but not while I'm driving."

The three of them walk away, leaving just me and Brooke standing in the dirt lot of Billy's. Brooke's blue eyes sparkle in the starlight, and I've never been so sure of something in my entire life.

47

BROOKE

I'm enraged with Addie and frustrated with Billy.

"Why'd you let them do that to you?" I hiss after Logan, Matt, and Melanie walk away.

Beck smiles gently down at me. "It's just Addie. She's not worth it."

"Seems like someone needs to put her in her place," I grumble.

"She'll end up stuck in the mud with no one to help her one day," Beck muses. "Come on, I have something I want to show you."

"You do?"

"Yes." Beck walks to his truck and opens my door.

I get myself situated, and he leaves Billy's behind, driving through the dark mountain roads to the sounds of old-school country music on the radio.

He's quiet, but so am I. I expect anxiety, but I don't have any. I decided to trust Beck completely, and my body actually got the memo this time.

He follows the road around twists and turns, and I can tell we're going up, but it's hard to see because of the Virginia pines lining the road and casting their shadows over us.

Beck reaches a clearing and parks. "Would you wait here for a moment?"

I don't know why he's asking me to wait, but I will.

I nod.

"And you'll keep your eyes closed?"

I scrunch them shut as he exits the truck.

"I'll open your door when I'm ready."

I lean my head back against the headrest while I wait for Beck. There's a scuffling and scraping sound, but then Beck opens my door, and the look he gives me is full of such tender care that I can't help but shiver.

"Cold?" he asks with concern.

"Not really," I say, but he wraps his arm around me just the same.

Beck guides me to the back of his truck, where the tailgate is down. A blanket is spread across the bed, and the stars overhead cast a canopy of lights against the inky sky. Before I can ask where we are or what we're doing, Beck lifts me up and sets me on the edge of the tailgate. He steps up to me and presses his lips against mine in a soft and warm kiss.

"Brooke," he breathes. "I have a question for you."

"Okay," I murmur back, closing my eyes. I try to lean against him, but a rush of cool air hits me where Beck was just standing. In alarm, I open my eyes and find that Dr. Beckett Whistler is down on one knee, holding out a ring in the palm of his hand.

"Brooke Belle Bastion," he says, his voice choked with emotion. "Will you marry me?"

I hop off the tailgate and crouch to be at his level. "Yes." I throw my arms around him. "I will absolutely marry you."

His lips crash into mine with a delicious promise, and it finally hits me.

"You smell like ginger."

"Uh … yes?" He holds his hand up in a guilty-as-charged gesture. He must have forgotten he was holding a ring, because for the briefest moment in time, it flies up, out of his hand, and I catch sight of the gold band and the red gem atop it in the starlight before it disappears. "Oh no," he whispers, his eyes growing huge. "June is going to kill me."

"Meemaw is *not* going to kill you," I quip back. "She's been wanting her grandbabies to get married and give her great-grandbabies for years. If anything, I think you are making her dreams come true."

Beck scratches behind his neck as he surveys the field. "Yes, but that ring was … really special."

"It's just a ring," I say, because truthfully I didn't look at it much; I was too busy looking at the man offering it to me.

"No, honey," Beck says, and the endearment is so natural on his lips that my heart melts. "That ring was June's mother's. It was the only thing of value she kept when she had to sell everything else to survive. The ruby was her favorite gem. It symbolized wisdom, virtue, and the blood of Christ. It's a part of your history that June kept for you. She wanted you to have it, and she wanted me to give it to you when I proposed."

Tears rise unbidden, and my throat tightens. "You asked Meemaw?"

"Yes. Of course I did. And your parents."

I can't see anymore because of the tears streaming down my face. "Does she know you're asking me tonight?"

"No, I told her it had to be on our timeline. I planned to wait longer, but there doesn't seem to be much point. It's you, Brooke. You're the one."

"Can we look for the ring now?" I ask.

"Yes, I'd really like to live to marry you, and I don't want June to use Ol' Eddie on me before I have the chance to call you my wife."

I giggle and pull my phone out, clicking on my flashlight. Beck does the same. I start to walk toward where I think the ring landed, but Beck's arm circles my waist, and he pulls me close for a lengthy kiss.

Slightly breathless when he pulls away, he whispers, "Now we can look for the ring."

He keeps his hand in mine as we walk methodically over the ground, searching with our lights.

Finally, I spy something shiny.

It's my ruby engagement ring, and it landed on a wild violet.

When we find the ring, Beck slides back down to one knee and slips it on my left ring finger. Before he stands up again, he presses a kiss to my knuckle. "Now, it's up to you to survive until our wedding day."

I laugh. This man who was so grumpy at first is unexpectedly wonderful.

Beck reaches into his back jeans pocket and extracts an envelope. The name *The Future Mrs. Brooke Whistler* is on it, but it's not in Beck's handwriting. It's in Meemaw's.

MEEMAW

ear Brooke,

I know I do things backward sometimes, but when you've lived as long as I have, you'll find backward, forward, sideways—it doesn't matter as long as you're doing what you should.

I've had this ring since my own mother passed. I saw her wear it every day, and even though things were not easy, this ring was a constant in our lives. The story of how it came to her is a long one, but you need to know that it's been passed down from generations. Still, when Mom passed and the ring was my own, it never felt like mine. So I prayed about it. And even though you were a little girl, I found that this was your ring, and I got to keep it safe for you.

Brooke, if God can make even the rocks this beautiful, then why are you worried? He'll make your life far more beautiful than you can imagine.

Hard times, pain, and suffering are all true. But so is beauty, truth, and goodness. You'll find that in your marriage.

I am so proud of you.

Love,

Meemaw

48

BROOKE

I'm engaged. To the most wonderful man I've ever met. I can't even think in complete sentences anymore because every few words, I remember something about Beck and get distracted. Being in love is like if all the light and goodness in the world was amplified tenfold. While I loved him before he proposed, he continues to surprise and delight me.

The light of the morning sun reflects on the ruby engagement ring as I sit on the porch swing and wait for Beck. I adjust the crochet blanket over my lap to ward off the chill.

The low hum of an engine coming down the road kicks my heart into gear, and when Beck's truck turns into the driveway, butterflies erupt in my stomach. Still, that's nothing compared to what my heart does when he gets out of the truck and hurries up the walkway to me.

Beck leans down and plants a gentle kiss on my lips. "Good morning," he whispers before sitting next to me and wrapping his arm around me. I lean into his warmth, his familiar ginger scent, and the peace that comes from being in his arms. "What are you doing today?"

"Getting a start on my Pinterest board wedding planning." I smile up at him. Instead of smiling back, he shifts and sets his jaw in a firm line. My hand flies to my hair as I ask, "Is there something wrong?"

Beck gently guides my hand away from my hair. "You have trichotillomania, don't you?"

I bob my head and don't meet his eyes because it's weird and I'm ashamed of it.

He tips my head up. "Don't do that, Brooke."

"I don't mean to," I start to say, but he interrupts me and squeezes both my hands.

"No, I meant, don't be ashamed of it. You're beautiful, and so strong and courageous. It's not easy to live with that condition."

"It's why I have pink hair," I whisper. "If I spend money on it, then I don't *want* to pull it out as much. I just do it now when I'm anxious."

Beck nods, his brown eyes thoughtful and understanding. "I wanted to ask you about something for the wedding. And it needs to be both of our decision, but…" He almost looks shy as he looks at me. "I was wondering if we could get married in a Catholic Church?" He takes a moment to look away before speaking again. "It's just that—I am Catholic, and my faith is important to me. It wasn't something Addie was willing to consider, so we were at the Baptist church, and I just … I don't want to give up my faith. But, if you want to get married at your church back home, could we make sure there's a Catholic priest there?"

I hear the sincerity in his voice, the pain that Addie caused, and I won't do that to Beck. Truthfully, I haven't been terribly invested in my faith lately. I've read my Bible a little bit more, but there's this sense of something missing.

"They make us wait and do marriage class stuff, right?" I ask, because I remember Connor and Paige's wedding and how they had to wait.

"Yeah, six months."

That decides it for me. I can give Beck a gift right now: I can prove that I'm not like Addie.

"I don't want to get married in Marquette in March," I say. "It's cold, snowy, and icy, and there could be a blizzard, and then we'd have to wait even longer. I want to get married here, to you, at whatever church you want."

Beck smiles before he slides his hands up my arms and pulls me in for a delicious kiss. When we break apart, I have one question for him.

"Could you please call to make the six-month countdown start today?"

Beck's low laugh rumbles through the porch swing as he kisses me again.

49

BECK

It's my last night in the E.R., and then I'm taking a week off before I switch to day shifts. This, of course, not only will be wildly better for my sleep schedule, but it means that I'll be able to spend time with my fiancée. Hiking with her, sitting on the porch swing with her, and definitely kissing her at any time of day. As we head into fall and winter, the idea of cozying up with her by a fire as the stars come out around us and probably not watching the fire at all is appealing.

There has not been a single incident this evening on my shift. It's midnight, so I slip into the break room to eat my sandwich.

Peony stands off to the side of the fridge with her sandwich.

"Hi, Peony," I say as I pull my own sub from the fridge.

"Hey, Dr. Whistler," she responds.

"It's Beck."

"Ummm." She chews her lip.

"What is it?" I ask, concerned by her unusual behavior.

"I was just wondering if, now that we aren't going to work together, you'd like to go out with me sometime," Peony mumbles to the floor. But then she meets my eyes with her own brown ones. "Oh. You met someone, didn't you?"

I nod, thinking of Brooke and how she's not just someone, she's the *only* one for me.

"You're seeing her?"

I nod again, because yes, I am definitely seeing her and intend to see her and only her until I die.

"Oh wow. You're engaged?" Peony asks as she stares at me.

I blink. "How did you know?"

"It's written all over your face," Peony replies. "You have that look men only have when they're thinking of the woman they're in love with."

"Are you some kind of love savant?" I tease, which is probably the first time I've ever teased a coworker in the history of ... ever.

"No, just highly observant at weddings."

"Sorry, Peony. You'll find someone."

Peony rolls her eyes. "Congratulations, Doctor Beck."

She excuses herself from the break room with her sandwich and leaves me to eat my meal in peace.

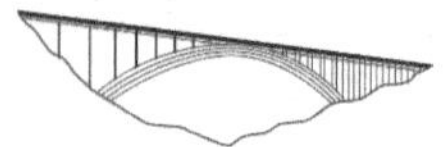

It's eight a.m. when I pull into the driveway between June's house and mine. I don't have to see Brooke on the swing to know that she's there, waiting for me.

I park, hop out of the truck, and hurry up the path to her. But she surprises me by running down the porch steps and launching herself into my arms. It's like a football tackle, but somehow better because *she's* the one wrapping her arms around me.

"Hi," she breathes.

I don't respond at all, I just lean down and kiss her. Thoroughly.

"I said *after* you're married. None of that *before*," June hollers from an open window. "Brooke and I made you fried chicken to celebrate."

When Brooke steps back, her blue eyes meet mine, full of mischief. "Why aren't we already married?"

"Six more months, love. Six more months."

Epilogue

BECK

Bridge Day is epic. But what isn't epic about it is that all these people are doing really dangerous things. I can't *unsee* the potential for an emergency room doctor's services. The BASE jumpers, the gliders, the people just walking across the bridge. Ok, the people walking across the bridge are fine; it's mostly the BASE jumpers that have my doctor senses on high alert.

No. I'm not on call today. I'm here on a date with Brooke, and I'm desperate to steal some longer kisses away from June's prying eyes, because whenever there's even the slightest chance of propriety being thrown by the wayside, June appears. She has some sixth sense about it. And honestly, maybe a seventh that is completely out of tune with what's actually happening.

Being engaged to Brooke means that June now feels it is her right to barge into my house whenever Brooke has been over for 'too long.'

The latest instance was when she pushed into my house at nine o'clock at night and found me and Brooke watching—*yes*, actually watching—a movie together.

"I promise I'll stop doing this once you're married in the eyes of God, but for now…"

And then she sat *in between* us on the couch.

I know her heart is in the right place, and it's hard to be annoyed with her when she clearly loves her granddaughter so much.

But also, I am annoyed.

Brooke and I walk hand in hand through the crowd, where I try not to notice the BASE jumpers launching off the bridge. It's the one day a year that the bridge is open to people on foot, and the views are spectacular.

Brooke doesn't like heights, and though I've known this about her, I also know that part of her coping mechanism for anxiety is to do things that scare her. Which is why, as we cross the bridge, we're actually on our way to a date that she might say a hard no to. I took a calculated risk and booked it anyway.

What's the point of living in a tourist area if you can't use touristy activities to woo your fiancée?

"Beck?" Brooke looks up at me from under her thick lashes.

"Yes?"

"Why are you rushing? I thought we were here to see the view from the bridge."

I scrub a hand down my stubbled jaw. I don't meet her eyes exactly as I answer, "We are."

We've almost crossed to the other side, and I spy Lynette holding a sign that says, "Whistler, reservation for two." Lynette recently started working at the bridge catwalk now that rafting season has slowed down.

Brooke sees her too. "Hey, Lynette!" she calls.

Lynette flashes a huge smile. "You ready for this?" she calls back.

"Beck?" Brooke questions. "What are we doing?" Then she takes it all in, and it clicks. "No. You didn't? We are? No way."

"You don't have to do it if you don't want to. But I've always wanted to try it out."

"You are securely attached to a harness the entire time," Lynette adds.

"There's no reason…" Brooke swallows. "To be scared?"

Lynette shrugs. "Nah, that's just your self-preservation instincts overriding the safety features. It's basic psychology. You have a physiological response to something you're scared of, even though your brain *knows* you're safe."

I grin at Brooke, whose narrowed eyes and squared shoulders make her look like she's about to march into battle, and not across the catwalk of the New River Gorge Bridge while wearing a state-of-the-art harness and clipped into safety cables.

"I don't want to be like Melanie and film everything, but Beck, if I'm doing this, please tell me you'll get a video. I will need documentation for posterity's sake."

"Whatever you want," I say, and I mean it.

Brooke flips her hair over her shoulder. "Ok," she says to Lynette. "Let's do this."

Lynette leads us to the launch area, where she helps us into our harnesses and clips us onto the wire.

There are other people on the catwalk, but it's not crowded. Probably because the bridge itself is open to pedestrians above.

Brooke inhales a shaky breath before she steps foot on the catwalk. I lean forward and whisper over her shoulder, "I promise I won't let you fall."

She turns so her eyes bore deeply into mine. "I think it's too late for that." She smirks. "You ready to film this? Because it's only happening once."

I hold out my phone and start recording. "Ready."

Brooke takes another tentative step. Her hands clutch the railing, but she moves forward, determined. After a minute of filming her inching across the bridge, I call out for her to stop. She does, and she turns to face me.

Standing there, framed in the backlit shadows of the bridge, high above the golds and yellows of autumn below with her long blonde hair dancing on the wind, a wide smile on her face, the headstrong way she faces her fears and refuses to let them master her, I've never seen anything more gorgeous.

"Can we sit when we get to the middle?" Brooke asks.

I nod. She could ask me for anything and I'd say yes.

When we get to the middle of the bridge, Brooke sits and dangles her legs over the side. I plunk down beside her, my own legs hanging off the platform. She leans toward me, and I loop my arm around her, pulling her as close to my side as I can.

"I love you, Brooke," I whisper. "You are the most gorgeous woman, inside and out."

Her response doesn't involve words. Frankly, I'm glad it doesn't.

No, her response is to take my face in both her hands and guide my lips to hers.

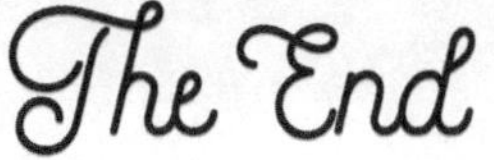

*If you loved this book, please consider leaving a review
on Amazon or Goodreads!*

Want to know what's next for Brooke and Beck? Find out in the newsletter exclusive bonus scene!

dl.bookfunnel.com/zi8xbwqfx3

Want to read Paige and Connor's story? You can here!

amazon.com/dp/B0F8HVCQ2R

Preorder *Shenando^ordon't ah*, Ben and Lynette's story!

amazon.com/dp/B0FK47Y2T4

Acknowledgements

Writing a book is a work of heart, and surprisingly, many hands. I would be remiss if I didn't first thank God for the gifts of creativity and imagination that make creating stories possible.

I also need to thank my family—Patrick, for believing in me and supporting my crazy dreams of being an author. Gabriella, Maria, Pascale, Blaise, and Paxton—you five children have an invitation to my party when I spit out my dentures on my 100th birthday cake, no matter what. I love all of you so much.

Caitlin Miller, you continue to amaze me with your kindness, encouragement, and grasp of how a story will work best. Thank you for being my editor. I'm so grateful that we crossed paths.

Benita Thompson, I'll brag about your cover design skills all day long. Sure we all know to not judge a book by its cover, but we also know, we totally all do. Thank you for making my covers eye-catching and beautiful and even better than I could imagine.

To my friends—Mary, Lily, Julia—let's write together soon. Amanda, Nicole, April, Beriah, Mary Kate, and Judith—thank you for being such incredible supporters of me and this dream.

To my internet friends—Madelyn, Ursi, Leah, Rachel, Andrea, Mary, Maggie, Rosie, Rebecca, Audrey, and all the ladies in the bookstagram academy, thank you for your encouragement, your kindness and your support. I'm so blessed to 'know' you. Let's get that writing retreat out of the group chat soon!

Lastly, (but definitely not least), to every one who has picked up one of my books—*thank you*. Your support makes a world of difference, and it is incredible that I can do *this* while raising five children. It is an honor and a privilege to create books for you to read, and I do not take that lightly.

So much love to you all,
Olivia

Olivia Hope McCarthy loves uplifting love stories where characters grapple with real life issues. It is her greatest hope that her books encourage readers in daily life while still pointing to something higher.

All of Olivia's romantic comedies contain some elements of Christian faith.

You can connect with Olivia on Instagram:
@oliviamccarthyauthor